CW00867173

Mills & Boon
Best Seller Romance

A chance to read and collect some of the best-loved novels
from Mills & Boon—the world's largest publisher of
romantic fiction.

Every month, six titles by favourite Mills & Boon authors
will be re-published in the *Best Seller Romance* series.

A list of other titles in the *Best Seller Romance* series
can be found at the end of this book.

Rachel Lindsay

INNOCENT DECEPTION

MILLS & BOON LIMITED
LONDON · TORONTO

First published 1975
Australian copyright 1982
Philippine copyright 1982
This edition 1982

© Rachel Lindsay 1975

ISBN 0 263 74088 9

Set in 10 on 10½pt Plantin

02-1182

*Made and printed in Great Britain by
Richard Clay (The Chaucer Press) Ltd,
Bungay, Suffolk*

CHAPTER ONE

THE doctor finished speaking and rested his hands together on the top of his desk. He stared at the girl sitting opposite him. She was so still that he wondered whether she had taken in all that he had said to her, and he was about to re-phrase it when he saw the glimmer of tears in her eyes and knew there was no need for him to repeat his findings. She understood full well the implication.

'I don't suppose there's any point in having a second opinion?' The question came from her with diffidence and before he could reply she shook her head. 'No, I'm sure you're right. I've felt it coming on for months.'

'Then it's a pity you didn't come and see me before.'

'Would it have made any difference?'

'I would still have ordered you to stop,' he said, 'but probably for a shorter period. Still, six months isn't a life-time. It will have gone before you notice it.'

'It's not as easy as that.' She pushed back her chair and went to stand by the window. 'I'm not a tortoise, you know. I can't hibernate for six months.'

'Surely you have a family—a relative or friend to stay with? I mean, you aren't destitute. You came to see me privately. . . .'

'Medical insurance,' she said, and gave him a wide smile.

Animation altered her features and the doctor was aston-ished at the difference, or maybe it was because he was looking at her as a person and not as a patient; and a very pretty person she was too. Small and slim—surprisingly slim when one considered her profession—with small bones, pleasing curves and the colouring of an English country lass. It was a long time since he had seen golden-brown hair of that particular shade; and not out of a bottle either but completely natural, as was the rose-tinged skin. She had a well-shaped but rather large mouth with a childishly short upper lip, and amazingly blue eyes, almost gentian blue. He had known a girl at college with eyes like that. He coughed and gathered his wits, wishing there was something more constructive he could do to be of help.

'Will you need to see me again?' she was asking.

'Not until the end of six months. I don't anticipate any trouble.'

'Will I definitely be better at the end of it?'

'Completely.'

'And no recurrence?'

'Not if you obey my orders. If you cheat—even once—I won't be answerable for the consequences.'

The buzzer on his desk reminded him discreetly that there were other patients to be seen and he pushed back his chair and stood up.

Walking down Harley Street in the direction of Bond Street, Sharon Lane marvelled that only a few hours ago she had still had the prospect of a career ahead of her. Now that career had gone. Only for six months, it was true, but likely to be for ever if she did not obey the specialist's stringent instructions.

No more singing until her vocal chords were clear of inflammation. Viewed calmly it did not seem to be the end of the world, yet it could not have come at a worse time for her. Her agent had managed to get her an opera season with an excellent touring company which, if things had gone well, could have led to her being engaged for their London company in the winter. Now she would have to refuse the offer and run the risk of having them think she did not want to go on a provincial tour. Even if she showed them a letter from the specialist there would be no chance of them keeping the job open for her. In a profession as competitive as this one, there were a hundred singers for every vacancy; singers as good as herself, if not better.

How was she going to manage for six months? If her illness had occurred last year she might have had a chance of getting financial help from the government. But her grant had come to an end and the teachers at the college would be

6

too busy with new students to concern themselves over someone to whom they had already said goodbye.

As she signalled a bus and boarded it, she knew she was being unfair. The professor who had taught her in the last two years would always do what he could to help her. Unfortunately he was abroad for the next six weeks. His son in Australia had unexpectedly sent him a return ticket to go there for a holiday, and he had left for Adelaide only three days ago.

The bus reached the Baker Street subway and she jumped off. It had been a ridiculous extravagance to take it; she must start to watch the pennies and the half-pennies too.

Riding the high speed electric train taking her to one of London's outer suburbs, she again gave consideration to her problem, and again could not find a solution. The trouble was that she had not been trained for anything except singing.

The train emerged from a tunnel and drew to a stop. She walked down the platform and up the moving stairs to the street. A wide suburban street this time, with small houses and neat lawns. A few moments later she pushed open the gate of a semi-detached one and, skirting the trimly cut path, went round the back of the house to let herself into the kitchen.

A girl about her own age was mincing something on the table and she looked up and smiled as Sharon came in.

'I wasn't expecting you home so soon. It didn't take you long.' She set her spoon in the mixing bowl and went to switch on the electric kettle. 'You look in need of a cup of tea.'

'A stiff whisky, more like it!'

'You know where the bottle is kept; help yourself.'

'I was only joking,' Sharon said. 'Tea will suit me fine.' She set out two cups and saucers and then helped herself to a biscuit. 'What's for dinner?'

'I made your favourite. Steak and kidney pud!'

'You spoil me, Anne.'

7

'Tim and I thought you would be in need of cheering up.' The kettle boiled and tea was made and poured. 'You still haven't told me the specialist's verdict.'

'It was what I expected. No singing for six months; not one single solitary note.'

There was a short silence during which Anne sipped her tea and tugged at a fair strand of hair that fell untidily down one side of her face.

Sharon watched her, thinking how little her sister-in-law had changed in the six years she had been married to Tim. They had been hard years too; with her brother being made redundant after the first one and deciding to start up his own business. It had meant a great deal of penny-pinching for them both, and only now were things becoming easier as several large stores started to show interest in the unusual record player he had invented. Success looked as if it were round the corner, but the corner had not yet been turned and she had no intention of putting her own problems on to their shoulders, no matter how willing to carry them those shoulders were.

'Six months isn't all that long,' Anne said cheerily. 'Think how you would have felt if it had been a year—or even two.'

'It might have been better if it were. Then I'd have given singing up completely and looked for another career.'

'You'd hate to do anything else. You've been mad about singing ever since I can remember.'

'And you remember a long way back,' Sharon grinned. 'You used to come into our house to borrow sugar. I never thought you'd end up as my sister-in-law.'

'The sugar was only an excuse,' Anne said promptly. 'I really came in to see Tim. I adored him even when I was twelve. But to get back to you. You don't need to worry about taking it easy for six months. You're perfectly welcome to stay here as long as you don't mind sharing a room with the twins.'

Sharon swallowed the lump in her throat, anxious not to show how moved she was. 'Thanks for the offer, Anne, but

8

I've no intention of hibernating, even though I'll be song-less! I'm going to find myself temporary work. I'm sure there's something useful I can do.'

Anne was about to reply when a loud bellow came from upstairs. 'My two angels have woken up!' she announced. 'I'll go and get them.'

Sharon ran upstairs to collect her nephew and niece, known to her brother as the unheavenly twins. At two years of age they were at their most demanding and needed constant attention and amusement.

'Ups-a-daisy,' she said as she hoicked them out of their cots and carried them down to the kitchen. 'Auntie's going to make your tea and then play with you in the garden.'

It was not until later that evening, with Tim home, the twins in bed and the supper dishes cleared away, that her future was again discussed.

'Being trained for singing doesn't equip you with a training for anything else,' Tim said. 'But if you would like a job selling things, you could give me a hand.'

Sharon shook her head. 'You would just be finding something for me to do. I'm sure it's possible for me to offer my services to someone who really needs them—if only I could think what service I have to offer!'

'You're pretty and well spoken,' Tim said with brotherly candour. 'How about a receptionist?'

'I mustn't work constantly in a closed or stuffy atmosphere, so that lets out a shop or an office.'

'What about gardening?' Anne smiled, for Sharon's dislike of spiders and worms was well known.

Sharon smiled back. 'It might be my only solution. Perhaps I could get a job in the country somewhere. The trouble is I hate gardening and I know nothing about it.'

'How about this?' Anne stretched out for the evening paper. 'I was looking through Situations Vacant and found something that might solve your problem.' She bent her head and read aloud. 'Housekeeper wanted for elderly active gentleman. Small house in country. Must be able to take entire charge while present housekeeper on sick leave

9

for six months.' Anne looked up. 'What do you think of that?'

'I'm not sure. I have no qualifications for running a house.'

'You're a good cook; you iron like a dream—the twins have never looked so smart—and you're excellent with children.'

'An elderly active man isn't likely to have any children for me to take care of!'

'Not unless you start giving him ideas!' Tim intervened, 'Anyway, I think it's nonsense for you to think of a job like that. You'd be bored to death.'

'It might be just what I need,' Sharon corrected. 'A job without any competition where I can relax. It's in the country too, which is important.' She held out her hand for the paper. 'Is there an address or telephone number?'

'It was put in by an agency,' said Anne. 'The Edge Staff Bureau, 44 High Street.'

'I'll go and see them in the morning.'

'Don't be too quick to accept it,' Tim counselled. 'You know the old saying about fools rushing in.'

'What about "He who hesitates is lost"?' Anne and Sharon said simultaneously.

Tim held up his hands in mock horror and said he would not attempt to argue with two females who had set their minds on something.

'Just make sure you take up the employer's reference,' he counselled. 'You want to be sure he's really elderly and not an over-active fifty looking for a young girl!'

The advice proved to be needless, for when Sharon went to the Edge Staff Bureau next morning, she learned that the job had already been taken.

'But we have many others,' Mrs. Edge continued. A buxom grey-haired woman, she appeared to run the bureau with the aid of a young girl and a battery of telephones.

'It has to be in the country,' Sharon said, 'and I wouldn't wish to stay for more than six months.'

'My dear, how honest of you. So many girls these days

promise to stay for ever and walk out after the first week!'

'I wouldn't do that. If I took a job I'd keep it—all things being equal, that is.'

Mrs. Edge scanned a ledger in front of her, muttering to herself. 'There's a position going near Hyde Park. A small town house. It belongs to a young bachelor: he's away most weekends but does a fair amount of entertaining during the week. He wants someone young and pretty and——' she frowned. 'No, I don't think I would recommend that for you.'

'I wouldn't take it,' Sharon said firmly. 'I want to be a housekeeper, not a bed-keeper!'

Mrs. Edge looked taken aback. She stared at Sharon intently and then, as though satisfied with what she saw, nodded. 'I think I might have just the job for you. It's in a house in the country; a gem of a place with plenty of other staff. It would be quiet in the winter, I imagine, but if you only want the job for six months then it would be ideal, because the summer is wonderful there and the house is always full of the most interesting people.'

'If they have plenty of staff, what do they want *me* for?'

'To look after a little girl of eight.'

Sharon's pleasure evaporated. She enjoyed taking care of her nephew and niece, but she knew nothing of older children. Besides, an eight-year-old who was probably extremely spoiled was an entirely different proposition.

'I don't think I would like to look after a child. The job you advertised sounded much more in my line.'

'I'm sorry you feel like that.'

'Anyway, as I told you, I couldn't stay longer than six months.'

'That's all they would want you for. The child is going to boarding school in the autumn.'

'So young?'

'She has no mother,' Mrs. Edge explained, 'and since she is an only child, Mr. Sanderson feels she would be better off with other children. He travels a lot in the winter.'

Sharon felt a twinge of unhappiness for a little girl who

11

had everything except what she most needed.

Seeing the look of sympathy on her face, Mrs. Edge said: 'Are you sure you wouldn't change your mind? Pailings is such a beautiful place and——'

'Did you say Pailings?'

'Yes. Do you know it?'

'I know *of* it. Everyone in the music world has heard of Pailings. It's like Glyndebourne—only more so!'

Mrs. Edge smiled. 'More so is right! I've been supplying Mr. Sanderson with his staff and with companions for his little girl for the last three years, and each season he sends me a couple of tickets to go and hear one of the operas.'

'Could you tell me a little more about the job?' Sharon asked. 'If you honestly think I could cope, I'd like to consider it.'

'Of course you can cope. The child is eight and somewhat precocious for her age. But then that's to be expected when you consider her background. Mixing with opera singers is an eye-opener for anyone, let alone a child. Mr. Sanderson is inclined to treat her as if she's eighteen, not just eight. You've never seen a wardrobe like that little girl has. If I——' she stopped. 'Now, where was I?'

'Telling me whether you thought I could manage it.'

'All you have to do is to take Margaret to and from school and keep her occupied during the weekends and school holidays.'

'It doesn't sound difficult.'

'It isn't.'

'Then why have you had to keep filling the post? You mentioned that you've supplied Mr. Sanderson with other companions for his daughter.'

'None of the girls left willingly,' Mrs. Edge said promptly. 'Mr. Sanderson always fired them.'

Sharon's pleasure evaporated again. She did not relish the prospect of working for a difficult man. 'What about Mrs. Sanderson?'

'There isn't one now.'

This made the job even less attractive. Yet the thought of

being able to stay at Pailings and hear great operas being performed in a theatre specially built for the purpose, of watching world-famous singers who fought for the chance of singing there for the summer season, was too exciting for her to dismiss.

'If he's such a difficult man to work for, perhaps *I* mightn't suit him either?'

'I was getting round to that,' Mrs. Edge said. 'It depends how musical you are.'

'You almost make it sound as if that could be a draw-back' Sharon smiled.

'It could.'

'I beg your pardon?'

'It could,' Mrs. Edge replied. 'You obviously know something about music, because you've heard of Pailings, but I——' she stopped. 'You don't sing, do you?'

'No.' Sharon's voice was firm.

'Thank goodness for that. The last girl I sent Mr. Sanderson apparently broke into song every time he came into the room! Of course she didn't last more than a fortnight, which was one week less than the girl before her.'

Suddenly it all became clear to Sharon, and she was struck by the humour of the situation. 'You mean he's been firing these girls because they took the job in order to get a chance of meeting him?'

'I'm afraid so.' The heavy bosom heaved and artificial pearls gleamed. '*You* wouldn't be going there for that reason, would you?'

'Definitely not. The last thing in the world I would do there is to sing.'

'Thank goodness for that,' Mrs. Edge pulled a phone towards her. 'I'll ring up and make an appointment for you to be interviewed right away. You are free at once, I take it?'

'Right this minute.'

'Excellent.' A number was dialled and Mrs. Edge had a short conversation before replacing the receiver. 'It's all arranged. I said you would be at Eaton Square at noon today.

If you leave at once you'll have ample time to get there.'

'But you said the job was at Pailings—in the country?'

'So it is. But you have to be interviewed first, and Mr. Sanderson leaves that to Mrs. Macklin. She's an American friend of his. He is so busy dashing round the world in winter and keeping the peace at Pailings in the summer that he doesn't have time to cope with personal staff problems. I've written down the name and address in Eaton Square, and the phone number in case you are delayed.'

'I won't be delayed. I'll leave at once.'

'Excellent, Miss Lane. I'm sure you won't regret it.'

CHAPTER TWO

DURING the journey to Eaton Square, Sharon remembered all she had heard and read about the Pailings Opera Company. It had been started as a hobby some thirty years ago by Paul Sanderson's father, and the son, having the same love of opera, had given the project equal devotion upon his father's death. He had outside business interests too, she recalled, which gave him sufficient money to maintain Pailings and its estate as his private home without having recourse to the revenue which the opera company brought in. This meant he could keep ploughing back the profits and continue to improve the facilities.

She had read an article about him some time ago in one of the Sunday papers, and though she could not recall it completely, little bits had stayed firmly in her mind: what had begun as his hobby had now become his obsession; he alone chose the operas to be sung each season and had the final say in which singers were engaged. He decided upon the conductor and musical director and had a tendency to bring back singers who were willing to remain at Pailings for the entire summer season; in this way he had managed to build up a remarkable group of men and women all dedicated to a high standard of production and a desire to in-

14

troduce opera to as wide an audience as possible.

From this desire had sprung the Pailings Touring Company, where singers of less experience but with great potential were encouraged to remain, on the understanding that once they had reached sufficient stature they would be allowed to sing at Pailings itself. But to be accepted by the Touring Company was as difficult as being accepted at Covent Garden or the Metropolitan, and Sharon had begged her agent to let her know the moment he could arrange for her to audition for Paul Sanderson.

'I would rather get you accepted by the Stuttgart Opera or one of the other continental companies,' Leo Horan had said.

He was one of the old school of agents: an excitable, hard-working man of Polish extraction who treated his clients as if they were his children, and shared their sorrows as well as their joys. He had received the news of Sharon's enforced absence from singing with as much grief as if he himself had been told to stop work, and had offered to give her sufficient money to tide her over until she was able to resume her career.

Though grateful for the offer she had declined it, unwilling to be placed under an obligation towards anyone.

'I have to stand on my feet, Leo,' she had said. 'It's important that I do; psychologically, I mean.'

'It's also important that you eat!' he had grunted. 'So promise me one thing. If you can't find the right sort of job, come and live with my wife and me. At least that way you won't starve!'

She smiled at the memory of his gruff kindness, and wondered what he would say if he knew she might be going to Pailings as a companion to the owner's child. It wasn't the initiation she had dreamed of, but it was at least getting her there!

The first thing to do was to make a good impression at her interview. Nervously she saw that the address she had to go to was an imposing block of apartments, and that the one she wanted was on the top floor. A penthouse, she assumed, though she could not imagine there being any worthwhile views to look at, unless one enjoyed rooftops. The thought of being able to spend the summer in the country was a wonderful prospect and she prayed hard as she pressed the bell.

The door was opened by a uniformed maid who showed her into a large living room. It was furnished with a blend of old and new that immediately established the American nationality of its owner. Small cushions in gay assorted colours dotted the two oatmeal-covered settees; a profusion of magazines were scattered on various small tables and some excellent pieces of American Colonial furniture were ranged along one wall: a gate-legged table, a writing desk and a narrow, glass-fronted bookcase. Beyond the windows a terrace was visible, the top of its protecting wall a mass of hyacinths in variegated mauves and pinks. Even through the glass the scent of them was in her nostrils, and she was admiring their beauty when she became aware that someone had come into the room—on the thick carpet it was impossible to hear any sound. She turned quickly and saw a woman in her early thirties coming towards her, hand outstretched. No old friend of the family here, Sharon thought, but one young enough to be more than a friend to Paul Sanderson. The fact that she interviewed all his staff and was now interviewing herself seemed to indicate this.

'Miss Lane? I am Mrs. Macklin.' The voice was fluid, with the curiously drawling vowels often heard in the Boston region. She indicated a chair and sank down gracefully herself. She was exceptionally tall and slim and so elegantly groomed that she gave an impression of beauty. But her brown eyes were set slightly too close together and her mouth, though generously outlined with lipstick, was thin. Her nose was thin too, with nostrils that flared slightly when she spoke, which gave her a nervous air despite her competent manner.

'You are much younger than I expected,' Mrs. Macklin said.

'I'm twenty-three.'

16

'You look less. I suppose it's because you're so small.'

Sharon immediately felt like a dwarf and sat up straight in her chair. 'I'm five foot three and quite healthy.' The incongruity of the two remarks struck her as amusing and she could not help smiling.

Mrs. Macklin smiled back yet gave the impression that she was not amused. 'Tell me something about yourself, Miss Lane. You don't look the type who would want to live in the country and look after a bad-tempered little girl.'

'I love the idea of working in the country. It must be lovely in the summer.'

'You know it's Pailings, of course?' The eyes were probing.

'Yes, I do; and if you're worried about my wanting to go there and sing, please forget it. I wouldn't give vent to one single note even if you paid me.'

'No voice, eh?' Mrs. Macklin relaxed and swung one long leg over the other. The creamy silk skirts of her dress swayed and settled around her. 'At least that's something in your favour. As Mrs. Edge has probably told you, we have already had quite enough trouble with stage-struck women. That's why I feel so guilty. I was responsible for engaging the last three girls and they all made such a nuisance of themselves that.... Well, I'm going to be extremely careful from now on. It means I have to ask lots of questions, but I'm sure you'll understand. This time I'm determined to engage someone who has no operatic aspirations whatever. A quiet, sensible woman who can cope with Margaret.'

'You make her sound a difficult child!'

'She is *extremely* difficult.'

'But she's only eight!'

'Only!' the woman exclaimed. 'Margaret is the most spoiled, rude and precocious child I've ever met. If she were mine, I would....' The thin lips came together in an unbecoming line. 'Still, she isn't mine and by the end of the year she will be in boarding school. Paul—Mr. Sanderson —has taken notice of me on *that* score at least, thank heavens.'

17

So Mrs. Macklin was responsible for having the child sent away from home. The faint, almost intangible dislike Sharon had experienced at her first sight of this woman became stronger. She knew that many children went to boarding school at the age of eight, but she herself had always deplored it; and not just for eight-year-olds either, but for any child. If parents were so bothered by their off-spring that they wanted to off-load them on to strangers for nine months of the year, then it seemed pointless to have a family at all. Aware that Mrs. Macklin was talking again, she hurriedly switched her thoughts back to the present.

'What other experience have you had, Miss Lane, and can you give me any references?'

Glad that she had anticipated these questions, Sharon nodded. 'I was head prefect at my school and was responsible for all the younger children at summer camp each year. I've never done this sort of work before because I've been—because I was at college, but recently I felt I wanted a complete change. I decided to try and get away from London and to do something entirely different.'

'Instead of working in an office, you mean.' Mrs. Macklin automatically assumed Sharon had been referring to a secretarial college. 'Looking after a child is certainly different from shorthand and typing. It isn't something you can put away in a drawer at the end of the day. A child is a continual responsibility and a weekend one as well. This isn't a five days a week position. During the season Mr. Sanderson has very little time for his daughter. That's why it's very important that we have someone who can take complete responsibility for her.'

'I'm sure I wouldn't have any problem coping with an eight-year-old girl,' Sharon said with conviction. 'I like children and I have always felt that they like *me*.'

'There is more to taking care of children than liking them. One needs knowledge and experience.'

Sharon frowned. 'Is there anything physically or mentally wrong with the child? I mean, she's normal, isn't she?'

'Perfectly normal. She is just extremely spoiled. For the

18

last few years her father has treated her as if she were an adult, and it's made her quite impossible to deal with. Believe me, my dear, you'll have your work cut out managing her.'

'I think it's a question of attitude, Mrs. Macklin; of building up a relationship.'

'Possibly.' The woman rose. Being a head taller than Sharon she looked down on her. 'I'll have to think about it, Miss Lane. I feel I would be happier with someone older and who had more experience. You're far too young and pretty to be contented for long with such a quiet life.'

'I didn't think Pailings was quiet in season.' The moment she spoke Sharon regretted it, for Mrs. Macklin's expression hardened.

'If you *were* given the position, Miss Lane, you wouldn't be mixing with the visitors. Mr. Sanderson likes to keep his personal life, and all those who share in it, separate from the opera company.'

'I didn't mean I would go out of my way to meet the people who work there or the visitors,' Sharon was determined to put the record straight. 'I merely thought that the singers who came there would be part of one's daily life.'

'That used to be the case a long time ago. But things are quite different now.' Mrs. Macklin moved to the door, casual and in control of the situation. 'The agency have your address, Miss Lane. If I should change my mind they will let you know.'

'Wouldn't you at least give me a trial?' Sharon's anxiety to get the post made her plead.

'I will think about it,' Mrs. Macklin promised without any reassurance in her voice, and Sharon found herself eased out of the apartment with a swiftness that indicated that it had been done many times before.

Walking to the main road she knew there was no chance whatever of the woman changing her mind. Instinctively she felt that the decision had not gone against her because of her lack of experience but because of her youth and

19

comeliness. If she had been in her forties or even young and ugly, she would not have been turned down. It really was the most awful luck. Not that looking after a spoiled eight-year-old was an occupation she would have chosen for herself in normal circumstances. But at this particular time it would have been ideal, keeping her in touch with the world she loved and a profession of which she was just beginning to be a part. If only she had been interviewed by Mr. Sanderson! She was sure he wouldn't have turned her down merely because she was young and not bad to look at; and she would have made it very clear that she had no designs on him. The thought of trying to attract a middle-aged widower was repellent, no matter how rich he was, and if he was as astute as rumour had it, then he would have been able to judge this for himself the moment he had seen her. But of course he'd never get the chance of doing so. Mrs. Macklin would make sure of that.

Sharon reached the main road. Ahead of her lay the B.A. terminal and beyond it the bulk of Victoria Station. Had Mrs. Macklin engaged her she might have been leaving Victoria tomorrow on a train bound for Pailings. Disappointment and anger merged into one indivisible emotion, and unaware of what she was doing she quickened her pace in the direction of the station.

It was lunchtime and there were not many people about as she went through the side entrance towards the ticket counter. On the platform nearest her a train was purring quietly to itself like a contented cat as it prepared for its outward journey. As always when she was in a station she felt a sense of excitement, and was reminded of the annual trip to the seaside which she and Tim had undertaken as children. How far away those carefree days seemed, when the sun had always been shining and the sky had held no clouds. Today the sky was full of clouds, and not one of them appeared to have a silver lining.

'Second class return to Pailings,' she said firmly, and thrust her money beneath the glass window.

Ticket in hand, she went to look at the indicator board.

The train for Pailings was already in and she would have to hurry if she wanted to catch it. She raced to the far end, had her ticket punched by the collector and just had time to find herself a seat in a second-class compartment before the train pulled out.

The journey took under an hour and would have taken even less had the train stopped at the village of Pailings itself. But it only did that during the season, for the convenience of the hundreds of people who attended the operas each evening.

Out of season, one had to get off at Haywards Heath and take a fairly long bus ride through the winding country lanes. This Sharon was forced to do. The buses were infrequent and as she had just missed one, she was obliged to wait half an hour for the next; she spent the time drinking undrinkable coffee and eating a stale sandwich served by a slovenly waitress in a café whose prices belied its cheap appearance.

Full, but still unsatisfied, she finally boarded the bus, looking around with interest as it wended its way deep into the heart of the countryside. Seeing the rolling green fields it was difficult to believe London was only a short distance away: one could not only be in another world but in another century. Thatched cottages nestled in flower-filled gardens; cows grazed on lush grass and the roar of traffic had given way to the whirr of tractors and the bleating of sheep.

The day was warm and the sun beat in through the glass, turning her chestnut brown hair to a glowing titian. Sharon closed her eyes and dozed, awakening with a jerk to find the conductor bending over her.

'You were the one who wanted Pailings, weren't you, miss?'

Smiling her thanks, she jumped off the bus and found herself on the outskirts of a small village. A narrow high street, marked by houses and several small shops, spiralled up a gruelling incline. In front of her was a small village green and beyond it the road forked, one side still showing

21

the back of the departing bus and the other curving so sharply on itself that after the first few yards it was impossible to see where it led. But a signpost on its corner showed the name Pailings, and she began to walk purposefully along it.

To her surprise the road was well kept, and as she breasted the curve she saw a pair of large stone pillars a hundred yards ahead. That must be the entrance to Pailings itself. She quickened her step, afraid that if she hesitated she might turn tail and run. Now that she was here, the impetuousness of her behaviour dawned on her. Mr. Sanderson might well refuse to see her. In fact he might not even be here! This second thought was more irritating than the first, and she wished she had had the foresight to telephone and find out if he was at home. Still, had she stopped to make the call, she might have lost her nerve and not come here at all.

She turned in past the pillars and found herself on a wide tarmac drive. Here there was another rustic signpost, one part of which had the word Pailings, the other the word House written in simple black letters. Assuming the latter to be Mr. Sanderson's private residence, she bore left as it indicated. The drive was beautifully kept, as were the lawns on either side of it. Even the trees looked as if they had been manicured. Huge beeches sent their branches arching above her head and as she emerged from beneath them, she had her first view of the house. It was everything she had imagined it to be: large yet not too large, its grey stone façade partially masked by green creeper, its windows glinting in the spring sunshine. She had obviously come to the back of the house, for in the centre were shallow steps leading up to a terrace which ran its entire length. There were several lounging chairs on it, but none were occupied, and she had decided to go round to the main entrance at the front when a little voice called out to her.

'What are you doing here? Don't you know this is private property?'

Sharon looked round but could not see anyone.

22

'I'm up *here*,' the voice said impatiently. 'Above your head.'

Sharon looked at the chestnut tree closest to her, and was able to discern a small figure perched on one of the topmost branches. Hidden by foliage it was difficult to see the child clearly, but despite jeans and sweat-shirt, she guessed it to be a little girl, guessed too that this was Margaret Sanderson.

'Is your name Margaret'? she asked, testing her assumption.

'Maggie,' came the reply. 'I hate being called Margaret. I suppose you're another one of Honor's hateful governesses?'

'Honor?'

'Mrs. Macklin.'

'Oh, I see.' Sharon hesitated. 'How did you guess?'

'Because you called me Margaret and she's the only person who ever calls me by that name. She knows I *hate* it.'

There seemed to be a lot of hatred embodied in such a little girl, but Sharon said nothing.

'Well?' the child went on. 'What are you waiting for?'

'I was hoping you would come down and show me the way. I want to go round to the front of the house. I've come to see your father.'

'Does he know? He never said anything to me.'

'I'm afraid he isn't expecting me.'

'Then he won't see you. He never sees *anyone* without an appointment.'

Sharon's spirit sank, but she refused to let it show in her voice. 'Perhaps you can help me to change his mind?' she said cheerfully. 'Do come down and show me the way.'

'I can't.'

'Why not?'

'Because I can't get down.' The little voice was suddenly plaintive. 'I'm stuck. You'll have to get the fire brigade or the police, otherwise I'll be up here for ever and die of starvation.'

'You do like to dramatise things, don't you?' Sharon laughed.

'What does that mean?'

'It means that you like to make everything more serious than it is. I'm sure there's no reason to call the police or the fire brigade. After all, you did manage to climb *up* the tree, and I'm sure you'll be able to climb down.'

'You don't know much about tree climbing,' the little voice said. 'I'm frightened to move.'

Only then did Sharon realise exactly how high the child was. The tree was an enormous one and the little girl was at least twenty feet above the ground. She had probably scrambled up with the agility of a monkey, but had lost her nerve when she had looked down and seen the height she had climbed.

Sharon glanced behind her, wondering where she could find some help.

'Are there any gardeners around? If I could find someone to bring a ladder. . . .'

'They're all at lunch,' the child replied, 'and I want my lunch too. I feel hungry and giddy.' The topmost branch shook as though its occupant was swaying and Sharon's heart started to pound. She knew she should run and get help, but felt afraid to leave the little girl alone. She was still hesitating when the child spoke again.

'Can't you come and rescue me? I wouldn't be frightened if you held my hand as I went down.'

'It's a long time since I've climbed any trees,' Sharon said, and since there was no answer other than an audible gulp, she dropped her bag on to the grass and placed one foot on the tree trunk. 'Hang on, Maggie, I'm coming up to fetch you.'

CHAPTER THREE

IT was amazing how quickly instinct and memory came to Sharon's aid, and more easily than she had believed possible, she found herself half-way up the tree. It was a lovely one to climb, with thick branches twisting off in various directions. It was not easy to climb wearing a dress and heaven knew what sort of state it would be in by the time she reached the ground again, but the most important thing was to bring down the child safely, and so she pushed on slowly towards the top.

'Maggie!' she called. 'Where are you?' There was no reply. 'Maggie,' she called again. 'I can't see you.'

'I'm here.' The little girl's voice was bubbling bright. 'Look down and you'll see me.'

Sharon hung gingerly to the branch and peered through the leaves; a long way down—much longer than she had anticipated—she saw a small thin figure with a pale triangular face and mousy hair drawn back into a plait.

'I thought you said you couldn't get down?'

'I could, I could!' The little girl danced round the tree with delight. 'Now you're the one who's stuck. I knew you would be and you can stay there for ever and ever! That'll teach Honor not to find me any more horrid governesses. She's an interfering old busybody and I hate her!' The head tilted and the piping voice stopped.

Sharon knew she was expected to show anger or fright—possibly both—and because she actually did feel both, she determined not to show either. 'You played a most ingenious trick on me,' she said cheerfully. 'It was an astute plan.'

'What does that mean? I don't understand such long words.'

'Don't you? You seem such a grown-up person I thought you *would* know.'

'I'm not grown up; I'm a child.'

'You don't act like one. All the children *I* know are kind and friendly.'

'Aren't grown-ups friendly too?'

'Not always.'

'I'm going to be friendly for ever and ever.'

'You haven't been friendly to *me*.'

'Because Honor sent you and I don't want you to see my father. I won't let her tell him how to look after me.'

'I'm afraid you've made a mistake about Mrs. Macklin wanting me,' Sharon said calmly. 'You see, she didn't. That's why I came down to see your daddy. I thought if I could talk to him myself, I might persuade him to take me.'

'I suppose you want to be a singer too?' the little girl taunted. 'They all do.'

'As a matter of fact I wanted to look after you, but I don't any more. The minute I get down to the ground I'm going back to London.'

'Why don't you want to stay here? The house is beautiful and there are hundreds of servants to wait on you like a queen. The last governess ate herself sick.'

'I'm sure the job is wonderful.' Sharon still kept her voice cheerful, though the swaying of the branch beneath her weight was beginning to make her feel somewhat nauseated. 'But not even being cared for like a queen would make me want to stay here with *you*.'

The little girl stamped her foot. 'You're horrible and rude to me!'

'You're horrible and rude to me too,' Sharon replied. 'And of course you've done exactly what Mrs. Macklin wanted.'

'How?'

'Well, she didn't want to give me the job, and now you've made sure I don't even want it.'

There was a long silence. Sharon resisted the urge to plead with the little girl to get someone to rescue her, for fear that her entreaties would make the child run away without letting anyone know she was stuck in the tree. She visualised having to stay here for hours and felt her hands grow clammy with fear.

'I never thought of that,' Maggie Sanderson said, and moved further out in the drive, away from the tree. 'If Honor didn't like you I'll *make* Daddy take you.'

'You have to help me to get down first. If you could find someone with a ladder and——'

'You don't need a ladder. I'll tell you how to climb down. Move back along the branch until you come to a fork.'

'Are you sure there is one?'

'Of course I'm sure. I live in that tree!'

The words made Sharon smile. It lessened her tension and she edged slowly backwards. As the child had said, her feet came to a point where the branch forked. 'What do I do now?' she called.

'Lower your right foot as far down as it will go—well, not too far down because you're bigger than me—and then you'll find a foothold.'

Gingerly Sharon did as she was told. 'What next?' she called.

'Do the same with your left foot. There's another foot-hold on the other side of the branch.'

Again Sharon obeyed. She was already half-way down the tree and her confidence was returning. In the distance she heard footsteps and, anxious to reach the ground before anyone came along and saw the foolish predicament she had got herself into, she moved more quickly than she should have done. The action robbed her of caution. Her feet slithered on the rough bark and though she tried to slow herself with her hands, she was not successful. She slipped, clutched a thick branch and then slipped again, falling in an ungainly heap on the tangle of grass at the bottom of the tree, right at the feet of the man who had just reached it.

Momentarily winded, she remained where she was, dimly aware of highly polished black shoes and a grey-trousered leg, before she gathered her wits sufficiently to scramble up into a more dignified position, knowing that nothing could make her look properly dignified with her linen dress crumpled and dusty and her shining thick hair sprinkled with leaves.

'It's too early to look for chestnuts,' a dry voice said without amusement. 'Or were you sitting up there to meditate?'

Sharon looked a long way up before she met unsmiling grey eyes. In an equally dry voice she said: 'I prefer to be comfortable when I meditate. If you must know, I was—I was. . . .' She paused, trying to control the sudden nausea that had gripped her. Unused as she was to climbing trees, the fall had shaken her more than she had realised and she found herself trembling so violently that she was afraid she would fall down again.

Hands came out to steady her, the fingers hard and digging into her arm. 'Don't you know better than to climb trees at your age?' the man asked in exasperation.

'She was rescuing *me*, Daddy,' Maggie cried.

The grip on Sharon's arm lessened as the man swung round and glanced down at his daughter. 'Were *you* up the tree, then?'

'Yes, Daddy, and she was trying to save me.'

Paul Sanderson drew a sharp breath. 'Was it your damsel in distress act again?' he asked in a quiet tone.

The grey eyes lowered and Sharon, a little more in control of herself, felt a stirring of pity. What a slight-looking child she was; more like an elf than a sturdy eight-year-old who lived in the country and who dined on food fit for a queen. She could not help smiling at the memory and the man turned to look at her in time to see it.

'I'm glad to see you have a sense of humour about the situation, Miss—er——'

'Sharon Lane. And please don't be angry with your daughter. Nothing was hurt except my pride.'

'Are you sure you're all right?'

He was eyeing her and she was once more aware of how dishevelled she looked. 'I wouldn't mind tidying myself,' she ventured.

'Come to *my* room,' Maggie cried, and gripped Sharon in a hard little hand, pulling her forward.

Sharon glanced over her shoulder at the man. 'I came from London to see you, Mr. Sanderson. It's about looking after your daughter.'

'You already seem to be doing that.' He did not move with her but remained by the tree. 'I'll see you in the house, Miss Lane, when you've had a chance to make yourself tidy.'

Happily she allowed herself to be led away. Paul Sanderson's home was as beautiful inside as out, with a graciousness that came from years of cultured living. Wealth was apparent without being obvious, indicated by the paintings, china and silver, and by the lustrous gleam of antique furniture. They went up a wide staircase and down a corridor to the little girl's bedroom. It was delightfully decorated with white and gold furniture, a flowered, fitted carpet and floral wallpaper. Several large, beautifully dressed dolls sprawled on the frilly white counterpane that covered the bed, and a huge panda sat astride a small buttoned armchair. Maggie, still holding Sharon by the hand, propelled her across the bedroom into a bathroom. Here again everything had been scaled down to a child's size, from the small bath to the low pedestal washbasin.

'What lovely rooms you have,' Sharon enthused.

'I hate them,' Maggie scowled. 'Honor designed it.'

'I think they're lovely. Why don't you like them?'

'They're soppy. I don't want a small sink and bath. I wanted a proper one.'

Bending low to wash her hands and tidy her hair, Sharon could see the little girl's point of view. 'It's exactly the right size for you,' she murmured diplomatically.

'I won't always be small,' Maggie Sanderson said primly.

'Of course you won't. But when you get bigger perhaps your father will arrange for you to move into another room.'

'Then this one will be wasted. My father will never marry again, you know. He'll never have any children except me. I wouldn't let him.'

29

'Do you have a towel?' Sharon enquired hastily. 'I don't want to use yours.'

'I don't mind if you do. You don't look diseased.'

Sharon hid a smile and dried her hands.

'You aren't very big, are you?' the little girl said, studying her candidly. 'How old are you?'

'Twenty-three.'

'What do you do when you're not a governess?'

Sharon ignored the question and returned to the bedroom. 'Would you like to show me the way down?'

With a toss of her head, Maggie led the way, put out at not having her curiosity satisfied. They went down the stairs and into a large, flower-filled room with an alcove at one end in which stood an enormous grand piano. Beside it was a table stacked with music sheets and a violin case.

Paul Sanderson was standing in front of a huge pink and grey marble fireplace, its colours echoed by the fine Aubusson carpet under-foot. The furniture had a comfortable lived-in look, though it was easy to appreciate that each piece was worth its weight in gold.

'Sit down, Miss Lane,' he said, and waited till she had done so before focussing on his daughter. 'That will be all, Maggie. You may leave us.'

'I want to stay.'

To Sharon's astonishment he nodded, and the child perched on the settee and kicked her legs backwards and forwards, watching them with the bright-eyed intensity of a bird. Paul Sanderson remained by the mantelpiece, in no way diminished by its size. He was younger than Sharon had envisaged, though he seemed old to be the father of such a little girl. She guessed him to be in his late thirties, for his dark hair was flecked with grey. It was even more grey at the temples and this gave him a distinguished air which went well with his cool and somewhat disdainful bearing. But there was nothing disdainful in his manner which, though controlled, was courteous. In fact, control was the word which came most strongly to mind as one looked at him, and Sharon had the impression that for many years he had exercised so much restraint that it had become part of his nature. The deep lines across his forehead and the ones etched down either side of his nose indicated suffering. It was not a good-looking face in the accepted sense of handsomeness; it was too lined and craggy, but it was without doubt a face to arouse one's attention, with its challenging eyes, firm nose and mobile mouth.

'You said you came here to see me about taking care of my daughter?' he began. 'I suppose Mrs. Macklin sent you. I'm afraid I didn't get any message from her.'

'I came here without telling her,' Sharon said quickly.

'You mean you wanted to see the job for yourself before making up your mind if you wished to take it?' he questioned. 'You're the first person who has ever done that. All the other girls we've employed jumped at the position unseen.'

'That's because they wanted to be at Pailings with you, Daddy,' Maggie interrupted.

'My daughter is right.' Paul Sanderson continued to look at Sharon. 'They came because they were either embryonic singers, composers or musicians. But if you've managed to get past Mrs. Macklin then you're obviously on the approved list!'

Sharon's conscience prickled sharply, but she ignored it. Later she would tell him the truth, but not until she had given him a chance to judge her for himself.

'I'm sorry I gave you such an undignified first impression of me, Mr. Sanderson.'

'I wouldn't count it against you,' he said kindly. 'You were at least trying to get my daughter *down* from the tree, whereas most of the people who have taken charge of her to date would have been delighted to string her up from it!'

'Daddy!' his daughter cried, and lunged at him with a happy shriek. He was momentarily caught off balance, but he steadied himself and patted her head.

'Rustle up some coffee for us, will you, poppet? I'm sure Miss Lane could do with some.' The little girl ran out and he resumed his regard of Sharon. 'I don't really know what to ask you. For the last few years I've left this sort of interviewing to Honor—Mrs. Macklin—and before that Maggie was looked after by my old nanny who has since retired.'

'I think I'd better tell you at once, Mr. Sanderson, that I have no experience of looking after children. But I told Mrs. Macklin I'd been a prefect at school and was responsible for the young children at our annual summer camp. I've also helped my sister-in-law with the twins—they're two now. It's different from having to cope with an eight-year-old, of course, but it's surely more a question of common sense than any specific training.'

'Perhaps.' It could not have been a more noncommittal word, though his next sentence gave Sharon more hope. 'She goes to an excellent private day school, so she wouldn't really require any additional teaching.'

'Then if it's only a question of taking care of her I really am capable even though I did fall down from the tree.'

His laugh was short. 'I don't hold you responsible for that, Miss Lane. I'm well aware of my daughter's naughtiness. I'm only glad you were intelligent enough not to let her know you were angry with her.'

'I was more angry with myself for falling for such a trick. I should have realised it's the sort of thing a bored eight-year-old would do.'

'Your generosity of spirit surprises me.'

She flushed at the dryness of his tone, afraid that he thought she was trying to show him how forgiving she was. 'I wouldn't always be so forbearing with your daughter, if I were in charge of her. But it's obvious she hasn't liked any of the women Mrs. Macklin has chosen for her, and she feared it would be the same with me.'

'My daughter isn't an easy child to control.' His voice was so cool that Sharon was sure she had said the wrong thing and wondered if he saw her words as a criticism of the American woman.

'Mrs. Macklin did tell me there'd been a few problems,' she said quickly, 'but don't you think that was because the girls you employed were more interested in you and what you could do for them than—than——' She floundered to a stop, but he did not help her and resolutely she ploughed on. 'I think they were more anxious to bring themselves to *your* attention than to take care of your daughter, and if a child senses she isn't wanted, she might try to draw attention to herself by being difficult.'

'A kind word doesn't always turn away wrath, Miss Lane. You may find that even the most psychologically guided approach will achieve no result whatever.'

'I would be surprised if an eight-year-old got the better of me!'

'But would you stick it to the end?'

'I believe the job is only for six months,' she said carefully.

'So it is. At least, I. . . .'

He said no more and she had the impression that he was not as committed to his decision to send his daughter to boarding school as Mrs. Macklin had intimated. Before the pause could lengthen into one which she felt she had to break, Maggie returned, looking self-important as she heralded the arrival of a young manservant with a tray which held coffee for two and a plate of icecream. There was no need to ask for whom the icecream was intended. Sitting herself down in a chair, the little girl began to demolish it with quiet ferocity.

'It's very rude to eat something without offering any of it to your guests,' her father said.

'She isn't my guest, she's yours.'

As before, Paul Sanderson ignored the rudeness and poured the coffee. Accepting a cup, Sharon sipped it. Much as she wanted the chance to live here and enjoy the music and study the singers, the idea of looking after such a horror was a daunting prospect, particularly if she was expected to let her go on behaving in this way. Had any of the other girls who had been employed here tried to improve her behaviour or had they been so concerned with their own future that they had given no thought to anything else? She sighed and kissed goodbye to all hope of staying at Pailings.

'You're suddenly quiet, Miss Lane,' Paul Sanderson said. 'Is there anything troubling you?'

'Yes, there is.' Sharon drew a deep breath. 'If I came here to—if you accepted me for the position—what authority would I have over your daughter?'

'I don't understand the question.'

'Am I expected to take complete charge of her?'

'Certainly. You will be responsible for taking and collecting her from school when the chauffeur is engaged with me, and I will expect you to be with her when she is at home. Does that satisfy your question?'

'Not quite. You see, I don't believe a child can have two different bosses.'

'I'm not engaging a boss for my daughter, Miss Lane, merely a companion.'

'I think your daughter has been trying to turn them into slaves!' Sharon saw the grey eyes flash, but she pressed on. 'I would prefer to talk to you in private, if you don't mind, Mr. Sanderson.'

The little girl looked up at this. 'I needn't go out, need I, Daddy?'

'I rather think you must,' he replied.

'But I haven't finished my icecream.'

'Take it with you.'

'I want to stay here.'

'No, my dear. Please leave us.'

The child stared at him and he stared back. Then she slowly stood up and went to the door.

'Goodbye, Maggie,' Sharon said pleasantly. 'I hope we meet again soon.'

'I don't. I think you're as hateful as Honor!'

'Maggie!' her father thundered. 'Will you get out?' The door slammed shut and he looked apologetically at Sharon. 'I'm sorry about that. But I'm not sure what's the best way of handling her. I alternate between being too easy-going or too tough.'

'Something in between might be better.'

'For that you need an equable temper—which I don't possess. I have a great many things on my mind, Miss Lane, and my patience isn't all it should be. I've given in to Maggie for too long and now she's thoroughly spoiled. That's why I've decided to send her to boarding school.'

'Does she want to go?'

For the first time his smile was genuinely amused. 'She says she'll burn the place down and murder the teachers! No, Miss Lane, my daughter does not want to go. But let's not discuss that. Let's talk instead about the job.'

'I would only accept if you gave me full charge of her. I promise not to smack her, but I do think she needs a firm hand.'

'You're welcome to have a go if you think it will do any good.'

'It's worth a try. Maggie is bright for her age; too bright, I think, and lonely.'

He looked surprised. 'There are always plenty of people around.'

'Children need other children. After all, it's the Easter holidays and it's a lovely day. You have beautiful grounds for her to play in, but she's playing by herself.'

'She knows she can ask anyone over any time she likes. The trouble is that she doesn't like any of the children at school. She refers to them as babies!'

'That's probably because she's rather sophisticated for her age. But I'm sure there must be one or two children she would have over if she were given the right encouragement.'

'And you believe you can give her that encouragement?'

'Yes.'

'Then do so.'

'You mean you're engaging me?'

'Hasn't Mrs. Macklin already done so?'

'No,' Sharon said. 'As a matter of fact I——' she stopped as the door opened and the woman they were talking about came in. Her arrival could not have been more ill-timed, and Sharon wished the ground would open up and swallow her.

35

'Miss Lane!' Honor Macklin said in surprise. 'What are *you* doing here?'

'Miss Lane felt she should see me before accepting the position,' Paul Sanderson interrupted.

'Before she *what*?' Honor Macklin looked furious. 'I never offered Miss Lane the position. She's quite unsuitable.'

The man seemed perplexed, and realising she owed him an explanation, Sharon said: 'Mrs. Macklin felt I was too young and too lacking in experience. That's why I decided to come down and see you myself. I know I shouldn't have done so, but——'

'I want you to look after me!' Unheard by any of them, Maggie had come back into the room and she now flung herself against Sharon and glared at the tall, thin woman standing beside her father. 'I *want* Miss Lane to stay with me. I want her!'

'When we require your opinion, Margaret, we'll ask for it,' Honor Macklin said in a bright voice. 'Now be a good girl and run out and play.'

'I don't want to go out and play. I live here and I'm staying here. *You* go out!'

'Maggie!' her father said angrily. 'Apologise at once. At once, do you hear?'

'No.'

'Kindly go to your room,' he said in the quietest possible voice, 'and don't leave it until I've been to see you.'

Silently Maggie went out, but not before Sharon had seen the pinched face and the pale grey eyes, so like her father's, shining with unshed tears. At the door the little girl paused, looking surprisingly small, and making Sharon suddenly aware that despite her precocity she was only eight, and a motherless eight at that.

'Do you mind if I go with your daughter, Mr. Sanderson?' Sharon asked, and without waiting for his reply, moved over to the door. 'I think I left my handkerchief in your room, Maggie. Would you mind if I went to get it?'

The little girl nodded, but not until they were in the

36

charming bedroom again did she speak.

'She won't let you stay and look after me. She'll talk my father out of it. She wraps him round her finger. Everyone says so.'

'You shouldn't listen to gossip.'

'It's true; and if it's true it isn't gossip. That's what Mrs. Goodwin says.'

'Who is Mrs. Goodwin?'

'Our cook. Goodwin is the butler.'

'Is that the young man who brought in the coffee?'

Maggie couldn't help giggling. 'That's Enzio. He's training to be a singer. I think Daddy is paying for it, so he helps out in the house.'

It was one way of getting staff, Sharon thought, and was glad she did not say so, for the little girl continued speaking.

'Daddy doesn't like Enzio working in the house, but Enzio won't listen to him. He says he has to pay Daddy back somehow.' The pale grey eyes were no longer full of tears as they looked round the room.

'I can't see your hanky. Are you sure you left it here?'

'It's in my handbag.'

'It's wicked to lie,' Maggie stated. 'Miss Williams said if you lie, your tongue falls out.'

Sharon bit her lip. 'Who is Miss Williams?'

'She was the last person who looked after me. Will *your* tongue fall out now?'

'Certainly not,' said Sharon. 'If one's tongue did fall out if one lied, Miss Williams would have lost *hers*.'

The child giggled. Her earlier antagonism had gone and she was completely friendly. If she had been a puppy, her tail would have been wagging.

'Can't you stop Honor from sending you away?'

'It depends on your father. And a little while ago you gave the impression that you didn't want me to stay.'

'I didn't mean it. I have a terrible temper, you know. It will be the death of me.'

This time Sharon could not stop herself from laughing.

37

'Did Miss Williams say that too?'

'Yes, she did. How did you know?'

'Never mind,' Sharon smiled, and picked up one of the dolls. It was beautifully dressed in white organdie and made her realise how untidy she herself must look. She put down the doll and went over to the mirror. Her dress was crumpled and still showed the dust marks of the chestnut tree. Her face was shining too and she took out her compact and powdered her nose: a small firm nose that matched the small firm chin. Not by any means a beautiful face, she decided, looking at herself critically; ingenuous was the best word and pretty was the most flattering one. But Mrs. Macklin would probably use far different words to describe her—high-handed and calculating being the most likely ones. Not that she could be blamed for being angry. It must have been an unwelcome surprise for her to have come in and seen the girl she had rejected that morning taking coffee with the man she had earmarked as her own personal possession. But I only want a job with him, Sharon thought. I don't care whether he's thirty-six or ninety-six.

She stood up and looked down at Maggie. 'I'd better go downstairs and say goodbye.'

'Can't you stay here a bit longer?'

'It wouldn't be polite.'

'If you don't come back and look after me, I'll run away.'

'That's baby talk, Maggie, not grown-up talk.' She went out, aware of the waif-like figure that leaned over the banisters to watch her as she walked down the stairs. As she reached the bottom, Paul Sanderson and his companion came out of the drawing room.

'Ah, there you are, Miss Lane,' he said. 'I've managed to convince Mrs. Macklin that you're not too young to take charge of Maggie. I've told her about the tree episode and we both feel it would be worth giving you a trial.'

'Thank you, Mr. Sanderson.' Sharon avoided Honor Macklin's eyes but felt their hard stare. 'When do you want me to start?'

'As soon as possible. Tomorrow if you could.'

'That would suit me very well. I'll come down on the morning train.'

'If you telephone and let me know the time of your arrival, I'll send the chauffeur to the station to meet you.'

She thanked him and he walked with her to the front door, where a dark limousine was waiting for her, a uniformed man at the wheel.

'The least I can do is to offer you a lift back to Haywards Heath,' her new employer smiled.

'I'm sorry to put you to so much trouble.'

'It's nothing compared with the trouble you're likely to have with Maggie.'

'I'll do my best to cope with it.'

'I'm sure you will.' He held out his hand. 'Goodbye, Miss Lane. I look forward to seeing you tomorrow.'

Sharon climbed into the car and resisted the urge to peep through the rear window as they glided away. When at last she did turn for a quick glimpse, the front door was closed and the house looked serene and shuttered. After tomorrow it would be her home. The thought was gratifying and she tried to stifle the memory of Mrs. Macklin. But the American woman refused to be easily dismissed from her mind, and remained below the surface of it, disturbing and strangely foreboding.

CHAPTER FOUR

ANNE and Tim were astonished when they learned for whom Sharon was going to work, though Tim was also perturbed that his sister had not disclosed her real background.

'I don't see that it matters about Sharon being a singer,' Anne protested. 'After all, she hasn't been engaged as one.'

'But if the man's so adamant about not employing anyone in his home who's interested in singing, he'll be furious when he finds out that he's been duped.'

'I intend to tell him the truth as soon as he's had a chance to know me better,' Sharon intervened.

'Then he'll throw you out on your ear,' said Tim.

'Not if I've already proved to him that I can look after his daughter. That's what I've been engaged for and that's what I intend to do. I couldn't turn down such a job, Tim. Most of my friends would give their eye teeth to be at Pailings.'

'With the opera company perhaps, not as a governess-cum-nanny.'

'They wouldn't care in what capacity they were there, so long as they were there. You have no idea what a place it is.'

'If you wanted to work in a stately home, I'm sure there are lots of other ones you could have chosen.'

'I'm not talking about the house,' she said impatiently. 'I'm talking about the opera company. They've got Batista Georgi conducting there this season. He's one of the greatest Mozartian conductors alive. Having the chance to listen to him is worth a month's salary.'

'I understand your reasons,' Tim muttered, 'but I still don't like the subterfuge. Sanderson is bound to find out.'

'I'll tell him as soon as I feel the opportunity is right,' she promised. 'I agree with you. It will be much better when he knows the truth, but I want him to get used to me first.'

'At least you won't do what some of the other girls he employed did. I can imagine how I'd feel to have someone warbling at me round the clock!'

'If only I dared warble,' Sharon sighed. 'I mustn't sing a single note.'

'Is there a Mrs. Sanderson?' Anne enquired.

'She died when Maggie was three.'

'How come he hasn't married again? He's rather good-looking from what I remember.'

'Do you know him?'

'Know is too intimate an adjective to use,' Anne grinned. 'Tim took me to Pailings when we were engaged.' She looked at her husband. 'Don't you remember him, darling? A tall dark-haired man standing by the piano?'

'With a hundred other tall dark-haired men,' Tim grinned back. 'Beats me the sort of things you women remember. You must have total recall.'

'Only when it suits us.'

'You can say that again! The last time you——'

'Don't change the subject,' Anne interrupted, and smiled at her sister-in-law. 'Is there a Mrs. Sanderson in the offing?'

'The American woman, I think.'

'Is she divorced or widowed?'

'I'm not sure. All I do know is that she's extremely elegant and capable and sees herself as mistress of Pailings.'

'Is she Sanderson's mistress already?' Anne asked with such avid curiosity that her husband muttered that he would leave the two of them alone to continue their destruction of character, and would be out pottering in the garage if he was needed.

As soon as they were alone, Anne smiled conspiratorially at Sharon. 'I think you've landed yourself a wonderful job. It could lead to all sorts of things.'

'My only hope is that it will lead to an audition in six months' time,' Sharon said firmly. 'I have no other motive in mind.'

'I'm sure you haven't. I was just trying to put it there!'

'Oh, Anne, really! Why would Mr. Sanderson look at me when he has a host of gorgeous females ready to grovel at his feet?'

'You're far lovelier than any of them.'

'You're biased. I'm an ordinary, fairly presentable young woman with a good singing voice if I go on practising like a maniac.'

'Your teacher said you had a great future,' Anne corrected. 'And he didn't strike me as the sort of man to say things he didn't mean. For heaven's sake, don't be modest. If you don't believe in yourself, how can you expect anyone else to believe in you?'

'I do believe in myself.'

'Then admit you've got a spectacular voice.'

'I've a very good voice,' Sharon conceded, 'but then so have hundreds of other women. You need more than that to set you apart from everyone else.'

'You've got more than that,' Anne said firmly. 'You wouldn't have been chosen for that touring company position otherwise. What's happened to all your ambitions? Don't tell me you've lost them.'

'I've put them in cold storage for six months. It's better that way. I have to resist the temptation to sing, and the only way I can do that is to stop thinking of myself as a singer.'

'At least that makes sense,' Anne conceded. 'I was beginning to think you'd lost confidence in yourself.'

'Oh, no. I still have confidence and I'm determined to succeed, but for the next six months I'm Maggie Sanderson's companion, nothing more.'

Sharon reminded herself of this as she bowled up the drive of Pailings in a chauffeur-driven car the following day. Even before the wheels had stopped turning, an excited little girl bounded down the steps to greet her.

'You've come, you've come!' Maggie cried. 'I knew she couldn't keep you away.'

'*She* is the cat's mother,' Sharon reprimanded.

'Honor could never be anybody's mother. She hates children and she hates me.'

'You seem to like using the word hate.'

Ignoring the remark, Maggie led the way into the house, followed by the chauffeur with two suitcases. 'Take them up to Miss Lane's room,' she commanded imperiously.

'*Please* take them,' Sharon murmured, touching Maggie's shoulder.

The child took the hint and repeated the order, with please as a preface. The chauffeur nodded and gave Sharon a slight smile as he did so.

'Now then,' Sharon said to Maggie. 'What about helping me to unpack?'

'We must have lunch first, and Daddy told me to apologise because he isn't here, but he had to go away for a few days.'

Sharon hid her disappointment; she had looked forward to meeting him again, though it was as well that she would have a chance to settle in first. By the time he returned she hoped to have established a routine with Maggie and also the beginning of some friendship. But she would have to tread warily. The child was too intelligent and too wary of strangers to have her confidence rushed. She could well imagine that as Paul Sanderson's daughter Maggie had come in for a great deal of attention and pretended liking. It would take careful handling to show the little girl that she was liked for herself and not because she was her father's daughter.

'Come *on*, Miss Lane,' Maggie said impatiently from the dining room door. 'I'm starving!'

Lunch was served in a small room off the larger one, though even this was twice as large as Tim's, with pretty Edwardian furniture and William Morris wallpaper and curtains.

'Honor decorated this room too,' Maggie announced. 'I like it better than my bedroom.'

'I'm glad you said that.'

'Said what?'

'That you liked this room.'

'Why shouldn't I say it? It's true.'

'Well, I know you don't—I know you aren't very fond of Mrs. Macklin,' Sharon said delicately, 'and I thought that might make you prejudiced about everything she did.'

The little girl considered the remark. 'Daddy likes me to tell the truth,' she said at last. 'He says honesty is the most important thing in the world. I hate Honor,' she said composedly, 'but I do like the way she did this room.'

Sharon bent quickly to her grapefruit and when she looked up it was to change the conversation, bringing it round to school and what subjects Maggie liked.

Lunch over, they went upstairs. She had been given a

43

room in the same corridor as the child's and, like the rest of the house, it was a delight to the eye. What a fortune this place must cost to run! Paul Sanderson obviously had a private fortune if he could maintain this place as well as run the Pailings Opera Company, for that surely took up all his time and left little over for personal business. Sharon hung her clothes in the fitted wardrobe that ran the width of the room and put her lingerie away in a bow-fronted chest of drawers, her every action watched by bright, bird-sharp eyes.

'What would you like to do this afternoon, Maggie?' she asked.

'Watch television.'

'It's much too nice a day to sit indoors and watch television.'

'I always watch it when I'm alone.'

'But you aren't alone. I'm here now. I thought we would go out and explore.'

'That's a soppy thing to do. I know all the grounds. It's boring to explore what you know.'

'Then I'll go alone,' Sharon said easily, 'and you can stay by yourself.'

The pert little face looked suspicious, as though waiting for some catch in the suggestion. But Sharon ignored the look and, picking up a cardigan, opened the bedroom door.

'I might as well go out now,' she said. 'Is there a dog that needs taking for a walk?'

'There are guard dogs,' Maggie said, 'but no house dogs.'

'Wouldn't you like one?'

'I don't know. I've never had one.'

Sharon was surprised that anyone should live in these beautiful country surroundings without having a pet. Her own and Tim's childhood, though spent in a small suburban house, had been filled with rabbits, tortoises and an assortment of dogs, cats and birds; even a pink mouse she remembered, and a hamster. She thought of the golden labrador that had been given to her on her eighth birthday and wondered how Maggie would react to such a gift. Yet if she

44

was going to boarding school in the autumn it might be better if she didn't have a pet, for parting from it could only add to the dismay that—according to her father—she was already feeling about having to leave home.

'If you want a dog,' Maggie said, 'I'm sure my father will get you one.'

'We'll think about it.'

They reached the hall and Sharon, without pressing Maggie to join her, went through the drawing room and on to the terrace.

'I'm going to draw the curtains and watch the television,' Maggie declared, 'and I don't care if it does give me a headache.'

'I'm sure you don't care,' Sharon said easily, and walked down the steps to the lawn. There was no need to ask whether Miss Williams was being quoted again. In the short time the woman had been here she seemed to have said a great many things to impinge on a young mind; most of them truisms though couched in a way to provoke immediate disagreement and disobedience. To tell Maggie not to do something was a sure way of having her want to do it. The only way she could be made to see reason was by being reasonable with her, and that required diplomacy. Sharon had no doubt that her diplomacy was going to be sorely tried and she determined not to lose her temper no matter how much she was provoked. At the moment Maggie was docile, but only because she was pleased that, in having Sharon look after her, she had exerted her authority over Honor Macklin. But inevitably there would be a clash of authority between herself and the child, and when it came she must be prepared for it.

For an hour she wandered in the grounds. They were so extensive that she knew it would take her several days to explore them, but today she was satisfied to wander across the lawns down to a small copse and to remain there. It was cool in the shade of the trees, reminding her that it was still only spring, and she was glad of the cardigan around her shoulders. When she was alone in beautiful surroundings she felt a tremendous urge to sing, as a dancer might feel the urge to dance as they moved over the lush green lawns, but though the music went round in her head she kept her lips firmly shut. Even humming was dangerous and had to be avoided.

At four o'clock, longing for tea, she returned to the house. Approaching it from the west side it seemed extremely large, and she realised that apart from Enzio who had served them lunch and the chauffeur who had collected her at the station, she had seen no other servants. It would be diplomatic to go and make the acquaintance of the housekeeper and her husband, she decided, and walked round the terrace until she came to the kitchen garden. It extended for some half acre and was bordered on one side by half a dozen large greenhouses. She glimpsed several figures in them, but only glanced at them briefly before pushing open a side door that led into a flagstoned hall. Various rooms gave off from it and as she hesitated, wondering where to go from here, a door opened on her left and a dumpy, middle-aged woman came through. She looked cheerful and the white apron enveloping her indicated that she was the cook.

'I'm Sharon Lane,' Sharon said quickly. 'Are you Mrs. Goodwin?'

'That's right. And you'll be the lady who's come to look after Miss Margaret?' The mud-coloured eyes were curious. 'You've come to the wrong part of the house. You want the other side.'

'I came to meet you and to introduce myself.'

Mrs. Goodwin seemed surprised and stepped back. Sharon pretended to take the gesture as an invitation and went into the kitchen.

'What a beautiful room!' she exclaimed, genuinely delighted by the air of hygienic efficiency intermingled with traditional farmhouse charm. The floor was covered with rustic brown tiles and the cupboards were of pine; working tops were marble and open shelves disclosed gay pottery herb jars and gleaming copper utensils.

'It was all new last year,' Mrs. Goodwin said.

'Mrs. Macklin did it.' Sharon made it a statement, not a question, wondering at the same time whether the American had had a hand in redecorating every room in the house.

'Oh, no,' Mrs. Goodwin replied, 'it was Mr. Sanderson. Cooking is his hobby. Not that he gets much time for it these days. But I've been complaining about the kitchen for years, and then climbing up to get something from one of the top cupboards I fell and broke my leg. I was in hospital six weeks and when I came home I found this new kitchen waiting for me.'

'You must have been delighted.'

'I was. Mr. Sanderson has so many things on his mind that I never expected him to bother with something as unimportant as a kitchen.'

'But it's the most important room in the house,' Sharon smiled.

'Most men don't know that. Still, Mr. Sanderson isn't like most men. He notices a surprising number of things. You wouldn't expect it from someone who's so busy.'

Despite a desire to learn all she could about her employer, Sharon said nothing, reluctant to gossip with any of the staff. Time would tell her all she wanted to know.

'I'm just making a pot of tea,' Mrs. Goodwin said tentatively. 'Would you care to join me?'

Sharon nodded and sat down in the colourful dining area, watching while the cook brewed the tea, cut several slices of a dark and rich home-made cake and then came over with it.

'How many staff are there?' Sharon enquired.

'Four living in and three women from the village. Not all that many when you consider the size of the house. During the season I have a kitchenmaid too. Mr. Sanderson gives a regular luncheon party every week for all the leading singers who are staying here, and many of them often come in for a late supper as well. Singers don't have a heavy meal

47

before they go on stage, you know, so they need something substantial afterwards.'

'It must be hard work for you.'

'It isn't easy during the season,' Mrs. Goodwin conceded.

'Do the singers live here?'

'Not in the house. They have their own block a few hundred yards away—near to the auditorium. It was built five years ago when Mrs. Sanderson was——' The cook stopped and sipped her tea and Sharon wondered whether she had been about to say before Mrs. Sanderson died.

Yet why should she look so uncomfortable and then stop speaking? Was Paul Sanderson not a widower, after all? Curiosity got the better of her discretion. 'Is Mr. Sanderson divorced?'

'Oh, no, his wife died three years ago.'

'I thought Maggie was only two at the time?'

The woman hesitated. 'Miss Maggie was only two when her mother went away.'

'I see.' Sharon did not see completely, but sensing Mrs. Goodwin's reluctance to continue the conversation, she allowed the subject to drop. It appeared that Mrs. Sanderson had left her husband a couple of years before she had died. Had it been because of another woman in his life or because she herself had had another man? Yet if it was for the former reason, surely he would have remarried by now. 'Does Mrs. Macklin come down often?' The question came out involuntarily, indicating where her thoughts had taken her and making her smile somewhat wryly as she realised it.

'Whenever she gets the chance,' Mrs. Goodwin replied. '*She's* divorced. Her husband was an American millionaire, I believe, but much older than her. She came to Pailings for the first time three years ago—as a visitor it was—and she was so taken with it that she's been coming ever since.'

'An opera-lover,' Sharon smiled.

Mrs. Goodwin's sniff required no further comment, and Sharon wondered whether she should have merely used the word lover. The picture it conjured up in her mind brought with it a vague restlessness, and she hastily finished her tea. 'I'd better go and see what Maggie is doing.'

'Still watching television, I bet. She's glued to that set.'

'So I've noticed. It's something I intend to stop, but I don't think it wise to start laying down the law the first day I'm here.'

'It's a pleasure to meet someone who'll use a bit of commonsense psychology with the child. None of the other young ladies did. But then they only took the job in order to come to Pailings and meet Mr. Sanderson.'

Guiltily Sharon wondered what Mrs. Goodwin would say if she knew that she too had aspirations to be a singer. Yet she could not imagine herself in ordinary circumstances going to the deception of taking a job as a child's companion in order to come to Pailings. She would certainly have done her best to see Paul Sanderson, but she would never have used a child in order to do so. Poor Maggie! Considering that for the last few years none of the people looking after her had cared for her, she was far less maladjusted than might have been expected.

Going into the small sitting room a few moments later, Sharon almost revised her opinion, for the child was lying sprawled on the carpet watching the television, a half empty box of chocolates on the floor beside her and several crumpled toffee papers scattered at her feet.

'You won't have much of an appetite for your tea,' Sharon commented.

'I only have orangeade and a biscuit. Then I have dinner with Daddy when he's here.'

'And when he isn't?'

'Then I eat what I like. Mrs. Goodwin makes scrumptious cakes.'

'You won't grow up to be a big girl if you live on cake.'

'I don't believe all that rubbish about eating your greens.'

'It isn't rubbish,' Sharon kept a smile on her face. 'It's been medically proved.'

'I don't know what that means.'

49

'There are lots of things you don't know, Maggie. I can see I'll have a lot to teach you.'

'You're not here to teach me anything. You're only here to see I don't get into trouble and to keep me company when I'm lonely. But I won't let you tell me what to do.'

'I won't let you tell *me* what to do either.' Sharon bent to pick up the box of chocolates, but Maggie was too quick for her and snatched it from her hands.

'They're my chocolates,' she cried. 'If I want to, I'll eat every one of them!'

'You'll make yourself ill.'

'I don't care.'

Sharon shrugged and in silence sat down. As she did so, Goodwin came in with a tray. On it were sandwiches and a glass of orangeade. 'Can I get you anything, Miss Lane?' he enquired.

'No, thank you. I already had tea with Mrs. Goodwin.'

'So she told me. She asked me to enquire at what time you and Miss Maggie would like dinner.'

'I don't want dinner,' Maggie interrupted. 'I'll have fruit salad and icecream—strawberry and vanilla.'

'Very good, miss.'

Sharon caught her lip between her teeth, trying to remember the sort of food she had been particularly partial to as a child. It was difficult to remember and probably pointless as well, since children's tastes were so different these days. She thought of the eight-year-old who lived next door to Tim and Anne and said aloud:

'Please tell Mrs. Goodwin I would like to have steak and chips. Nothing to begin with, just steak and chips and some jam pancakes to follow.'

If the butler was surprised at the choice, he hid it admirably and went solemnly from the room.

Maggie looked at Sharon, waiting for a comment about the icecream, but when nothing was said, she lay down on the floor again and went on watching the television. The cartoons had long since finished and a dull documentary was on the screen. It was nothing to hold the interest of a child and Sharon had the distinct feeling that Maggie was only watching it in order to be told to switch it off.

'If you're going to watch this boring programme,' Sharon said, 'perhaps you won't mind if I go and do something more interesting?'

'I don't care what you do.' The tip-tilted profile didn't move an inch, but as Sharon reached the door a piping voice said: 'What are you going to do?'

'Cut out a dress for myself.'

'A dress?' The little girl jumped to her feet. 'What sort of dress?'

'Something to wear in the evening.'

'What colour is it?'

'Blue with green flowers.'

'Can I come and watch you cut it out?'

'I thought you were watching television.'

'It's boring. I'd much rather watch you.'

Sharon nodded, and with Maggie beside her she went to her bedroom and set out the paper pattern on the floor. Not sure how she would occupy herself in the evenings, she had brought several lengths of fabric with her, and was glad she had done so, for it seemed that this was the way to arouse Maggie's interest. The little girl was exclaiming with delight at the variety of materials she glimpsed in the half-opened drawer, and she took out several lengths and draped them around her, posturing in front of the mirror in a way that was amusing as well as endearing. For all her grown-up ways, she was still such a child.

'Do you like clothes?' Sharon asked.

'I don't like the ones Honor buys for me. But when Daddy lets me buy my own, I love it.'

'What sort of things do you like?'

'Jeans and shirts. I hate soppy dresses.'

Maggie stuffed the material back into the drawer and raced from the room, returning with a ruby velvet dress with a lace-trimmed bodice and sleeves edged with lace and ribbon. It was a Victorian style dress of the kind Sharon had frequently seen in American magazines, and was not

51

the style she would herself have chosen for Maggie, who she felt required a far more simple kind of dressing. Evidently the little girl thought so too, for she tossed the garment on the bed and scowled at it.

'Honor bought it for me last week, but I'm never going to wear it.'

'I think it's a pretty dress. Perhaps if we take off the lace and ribbon you might like it better.'

Maggie's pale eyes narrowed suspiciously, as though she was unsure if Sharon meant what she said. 'Won't we spoil it if we do that?'

'If you dislike it so much and you won't wear it, the dress is going to be wasted anyway.'

Understanding the logic, Maggie nodded. 'Let's do it now. You can cut out your dress later.'

Sharon sat on the bed and carefully set to work, Maggie watching her, and sensing that the child would soon grow bored with this, Sharon gave her a loose edge of the lace to hold and instructed her to pull at it gently.

'That will make it easier for me to undo it,' she explained, and went on snipping.

Slowly the lace and ribbon was removed. It left surprisingly few marks on the dress and Sharon carried it into the bathroom and hung it over the shower rail.

'Why are you doing that?' Maggie asked.

'Steam is the best way to remove creases from velvet. We'll leave the dress hanging up here for a couple of days. After I've had a few baths, the velvet will look like new.'

'It's much better without the lace. I'll wear it when Daddy comes home. He'll be ever so surprised, because I told him I hated it.'

'I'm sure he'll be delighted to see you've changed your mind, especially as Mrs. Macklin bought it for you.'

'It wasn't a *present* from her,' Maggie said scathingly. 'Daddy gave her the money. He's always giving her money. Every time she comes down she gives him bills.'

'That's because she buys lots of things for you,' Sharon said hastily, and sought for a way of changing the subject.

'I think we have time to cut out my dress before supper, then I'll be able to tack it afterwards.'

Once more the two of them set to work. The child displayed an extraordinary aptitude with the material and seemed to know instinctively how to lay the pattern on it. She watched intently as Sharon cut it out and pinned the pieces together, and could hardly be persuaded to go off and have her bath.

'Can I stay up after supper and watch you sew it?'

'It will be far too late.'

'I never go to bed early. If I want to stay up and watch you, I will.'

Like a summer storm Maggie's temper had risen, but Sharon refused to let herself be disquieted. 'I think you should be in bed not later than nine o'clock, but if you want to stay up you'll have to stay on your own. I intend to go to my room at that time.'

'You mean you'll leave me alone downstairs?'

'If that's where you want to be.'

'How odd,' Maggie said in a most adult voice, and giving a giggle, skipped from the room.

Sharon heaved a sigh of relief, not sure who had come out best from the day so far. It looked as if the score was even at the moment, though by tonight it could well be a different story.

Seeing the look on Maggie's face as Goodwin set the dinner on the serving table at seven-thirty that evening, Sharon knew that the battle of wills between herself and the child was just beginning. In a cut glass bowl reposed a mountain of strawberry and vanilla icecream surrounded by a ring of assorted fresh fruit: hothouse peaches, grapes, nectarines and rings of fresh pineapple; a luxury fruit salad indeed. Yet Maggie had eyes only for the succulent-looking steak that rested on a bed of watercress and was ringed by golden crisp chips.

'We'll serve ourselves, Goodwin,' Sharon said, and waited until he had left the room before she helped herself to the steak.

53

'I would like some of those chips,' Maggie said. '*And* the steak.'

'I'm afraid there's only enough for one.' Sharon tipped all the chips—far more than she knew she would be able to eat—on to her plate and then took it over to the table. 'You have the supper you ordered,' she said over her shoulder. 'Do help yourself.'

'That's just a sweet. I want some steak. I love steak and chips.'

'Then you'd better order yourself some for tomorrow.'

'I want it now—*tonight*—I'm hungry.'

'Then you'll have to fill up on bread and butter.'

'I don't want bread and butter!'

'Then eat the icecream and fruit.'

'I hate icecream and fruit!' Maggie dashed over to the wall and pressed her finger to the bell, keeping it pressed down until Goodwin appeared in the doorway. 'Tell Cook I want steak and chips,' she ordered. 'Lots of chips!'

Goodwin glanced at Sharon and correctly interpreted her look. 'I'm afraid that will be impossible, Miss Maggie. The steak is in the freezer and it will take several hours to defrost.'

The child glanced from one adult to the other, uncertain what to do at this unexpected turn of events. 'I'm hungry,' she announced, 'and I want something to eat.'

'How about an omelette?' Sharon suggested, weakening from her original plan.

'I hate omelettes,' Maggie said mutinously. 'I want steak or nothing.'

'It looks as if it will have to be nothing,' Sharon replied composedly, and signalled Goodwin to leave.

He did so, and Maggie remained by the sideboard, not sure whether to eat the food that had been prepared for her or to maintain her stand and eat nothing. Sharon went on with her meal, though it was an effort to swallow the food and she longed to cut her steak in half and put it on a separate plate with some chips. But to do this would be defeating her own end, and knowing that weakness would not bring Maggie to heel, she determinedly went on eating.

'You can share my jam pancakes if you wish,' she said quietly.

'I'm not hungry for jam pancakes.'

Sharon stared at her plate and sighed. 'Come and sit down and I'll give you some of my chips.'

Suspiciously the little girl came towards the table, watching as Sharon carefully divided the chips off her plate and on to the empty one.

'You're giving me half,' Maggie said.

'I'm taking pity on you because you're hungry,' Sharon replied. 'But next time you order such a silly supper as icecream and fruit, you'll have to make do with it.'

'Are you going to share your steak with me too?'

'No.' Sharon was anxious to cling to the last shred of her determination, for she had already given in more than she had intended to do. 'Just the chips; and if you don't sit down and eat them right away, I'll change my mind about that.'

'No, you won't,' Maggie said, 'you're too kind.' She perched on her chair and picked up her fork. Her feet did not quite reach the carpet but dangled above it, making Sharon again realise that for all her big talk she was still only an eight-year-old.

'I'll get Mrs. Goodwin to make me steak and chips tomorrow,' Maggie announced as, plate empty, she pushed it away. 'Then we can both eat the same thing.'

'I don't think I want steak and chips two nights in a row,' Sharon replied. 'I thought I would ask Mrs. Goodwin what suggestions she had for supper.'

'She's a very good cook. When Daddy is here, he leaves all the menus to her.'

'Then I'll do the same, though it might be better if we had our main meal at lunchtime.'

'Not when Daddy is here,' Maggie said at once. 'I have dinner with him each night. I won't let you stop me doing that.'

'I have no intention of stopping you doing anything with

55

your father, and if he has no objection to your dining so late——'

'Well, he hasn't, he hasn't!' The little voice rose high, and then as Sharon remained quiet, it lowered. 'Why don't you tell me not to shout?'

'Because you'd shout all the more.'

Maggie giggled, but stopped as Goodwin came in with the pancakes. The rest of the meal went off without incident. They shared the pancakes between them and then returned to the sitting room where Maggie at once switched on the television and flung herself on the floor. Sharon watched too, but at nine o'clock she announced that she was going to bed. Maggie looked as though she were about to argue, but Sharon did not give her a chance and walked out of the room.

'Wait for me!' the child called, and ran after her. 'Are you going to sew your dress now?'

'Probably.'

'May I watch you?'

'No, it's too late.'

'Are you telling me to go to bed?'

'I'm not telling you anything. I would like you to go to bed, but I'll let you do as you wish.' Sharon paused by the door of her bedroom. 'Goodnight, dear. Sleep well.' She bent quickly and kissed the pale cheek. She felt it tense beneath her lips, but the child did not draw back, merely remained motionless as Sharon straightened and went into her room.

There was no sound outside in the corridor and she stood for a moment, listening. But the carpet was too thick for her to hear footsteps and she went over to the dressing table and picked up the pieces of fabric. She would not do any sewing tonight. If she left it for the morning and did it outside in the garden, it might encourage Maggie to sit there with her. Or better still, she would leave it until the afternoon. It would be one way of trying to compete with the television. Smiling happily at the plan, she undressed.

As she had expected, the bed was posture-sprung and

gave deliciously beneath her weight. Like everything in the house, it was of the best quality. In fact the only thing lacking here was a woman to take control. Still, the house seemed to run on oiled wheels and if its master was in need of a hostess there were no doubt plenty of women eager to oblige, not the least of them being Honor Macklin. How furious the American had been to see her at Pailings yesterday. Sharon smiled. She felt no guilt at going over the woman's head. Had the previous girls employed here been adequately trained to take care of a child, she could have understood her own application being turned down. But they had had no more experience than herself, and her rejection had been solely due to jealousy of her youth and freshness. How silly of Honor Macklin to be so jealous of Paul Sanderson's attention. He might be an excellent catch as a husband from a monetary standpoint, but he certainly wasn't from an emotional one. A woman would only be second best in his life. The Pailings Opera Company came first, and this was most likely the reason why his wife had left him.

I must stop thinking of Paul Sanderson, she decided. I'm here to look after his daughter. Yet even as she gave herself this order she knew she would never be able to carry it out. Come what may, Paul Sanderson was firmly fixed in her mind. Not because of his attraction as a man but because of Pailings and what opera meant to her life and future.

CHAPTER FIVE

By the end of the week Sharon felt she had been at Pailings for years. Life here was a luxury compared with life in her brother's semi-detached house. How much better it was to have a bathroom to oneself instead of having to share it with anyone else; to have unlimited hot water at all hours of the day and night and silent, efficient staff who took care of one's needs without being told what to do.

57

There were a few contretemps with Maggie, the most serious being on the third day after her arrival, when the child disappeared for several hours in the afternoon. Roaming the extensive grounds to look for her, Sharon had come upon the lake and seen a gay rubber ball floating in the middle of it. For a frozen instant of horror she thought that Maggie had gone in to retrieve it and got caught in the reeds, and had been on the verge of jumping into the water when she caught a glimpse of a thin little figure running through the trees. The sight of it had made her return to the house, where she had remained on the terrace until the child appeared more than an hour later, scuttling her way defiantly across the grass and pretending she did not know that Sharon had been desperately looking for her.

'If you disappear like that again,' Sharon said softly, 'I will confine you to your room for a day and not allow you out of the house for a week.'

'You wouldn't dare!'

'I don't make idle threats. I'm responsible for your safety and I will not have you playing cruel and thoughtless tricks on me.'

After this, Maggie gave the impression of settling down. In the days that followed she was docile and friendly, particularly so when Sharon let her help with the cutting out of another dress. The child's prowess in this field was remarkable, and on Friday morning the two of them went to Haywards Heath to search for a dress pattern and material for Maggie to make something for herself. It seemed a good way of encouraging her to wear dresses, and though she professed to prefer jeans, Sharon was sure that if she was allowed to choose a style for herself, she could be persuaded away from the inevitable denim.

An hour's hard search in a local store produced several lengths of assorted cotton material and a couple of simple dress patterns, and Maggie chattered excitedly about what she was going to make as they made their way back to the bus stop. It was near the railway station and occasionally a rush of people would emerge as a train arrived. As it was midday all the business men had left for town, and for the most part the travellers were women taking local journeys. But as Sharon and Maggie reached the head of the bus queue a large group of people—men as well as women—came out of the station. Several of them had startling tans and a few of the women were so elegantly dressed that they were immediately noticeable as foreigners. Porters were busy trundling cases and trunks and there was soon a sizeable amount of luggage stacked on the pavement.

'They're all going to Pailings,' Maggie commented casually. 'Daddy told me they would be arriving this weekend.'

Sharon's heart thumped in her chest. If the rehearsals were already beginning then these must be the first of the singers. With a few members of the orchestra too, she amended, glancing at a knot of earnest men hovering over a pile of musical instruments.

'It's a pity they didn't get the train to stop at Pailings' junction,' Sharon said.

'The train only stops there in the season for visitors. Singers aren't visitors, you know. They're workers.'

'Is that what your daddy says?'

Maggie nodded. 'He says he can't stand prima-prima——'

'Prima donnas,' Sharon volunteered.

'That's right. So he says everyone must be treated in the same way—as workers.'

'I agree with your father. Because a person can sing it doesn't make them different from anyone else. A beautiful voice is a gift from God, and one should be grateful for it, not proud.'

'You sound like the vicar!'

Sharon laughed. 'You'd better not tell him.'

Two large station-wagons drew up outside the station and the porters began to pile the luggage into the first one. The men and women clambered inside the second, and a thin young man who seemed to be in charge stood by the front counting everybody.

'That's Pickett,' Maggie said, and Sharon was annoyed

59

for not having recognised their chauffeur.

'I can't see the car,' she murmured.

'He came in one of the station-wagons. During the season he always meets the singers when they arrive.' Maggie caught Sharon's hand. 'Let's go back with them.'

'There might not be any room.'

'I'm sure there is.'

Sharon hesitated, strangely reluctant to go over and join the group. It was easy for her to maintain indifference to the world of opera so long as she held herself aloof from it, but she was not sure if she would be able to maintain this attitude if she mingled with the singers and musicians who were going to live here. Yet she had to put herself to the test, for with rehearsals beginning and the season approaching, she would not be able to avoid contact for ever.

'Pickett!' Maggie yelled. 'Can we go back with you?'

The chauffeur looked across the road and nodded, and grabbing Sharon by the hand, Maggie pulled her out of the queue and over to the station-wagon.

'We're just leaving,' the chauffeur greeted them, and lifted Maggie up the steps and into the car.

Sharon followed and saw her charge skipping down the aisle, saying hello to several men and women whom she recognised. Beneath her feet the floor trembled and Sharon took the first seat available and found herself next to a woman in her late thirties.

'I'm the rehearsal pianist,' the woman smiled. 'I take it you look after Maggie?'

'Yes. I've only been here a week.'

'Are you a would-be singer too?'

'I'm here to look after Maggie,' Sharon repeated.

'You'll be the first one who's done that for a long time,' came the dry reply.

'You talk as if you're a regular?'

'I've been coming here for the past five years.'

'Then you knew Mrs. Sanderson?'

The woman looked at her so quizzically that Sharon felt duty bound to explain herself. 'You can't blame me for being curious about Maggie's mother. She never talks about her and I'm not sure how much she remembers of her. But I do feel it's unhealthy not to refer to her at all.'

'Mrs. Sanderson left Pailings the season before I started to come down, so I never had a chance of seeing her for myself. She was extremely beautiful, I believe, and had no time for her daughter. According to everyone who knew her, she was only concerned with her career. That was the reason the marriage broke up.'

Though Sharon kept her features composed, she was listening avidly. The pianist was disclosing a mountain of information, most of it hearsay, of course, but since it stemmed from the other members of the company its origins were obviously based on fact rather than conjecture.

'Did she ever sing at Pailings?'

'That was how she met Mr. Sanderson. If you're an opera fan you may have heard her records. Helga Lindstrom?'

'Of course.' Sharon was astonished. 'She was quite well known. Swedish, wasn't she?'

'That's right. But she sang all over the world. She came here for a Mozart season and I don't think she ever went back to Sweden—at least not till her marriage broke up.'

'It's strange that she went away and left Maggie. I can understand a woman leaving her husband, but not her child.'

'It depends on one's financial position, I suppose.'

'Even so . . .'

'Anyway,' the pianist resumed, 'some women aren't maternal.'

The car slowed down as they went through the village of Pailings and then veered left at the end of the High Street. Sharon saw the two familiar signposts, and the car took the one that pointed right, crunching down the tarmacked drive that wound away from the house. She had not yet explored this part of the estate and she looked through the window with curiosity. Above the tips of the trees she caught an occasional glimpse of Pailings itself, but she could not see more than the chimneys and part of the roof. Yet as the crow flew it was not far away, merely so well screened by trees that it gave the impression of distance. The new building that housed accommodation for the company was built in the same medieval style: a mixture of brick and timber so weatherbeaten that it blended into the countryside. The theatre lay to the left of this, and was approached through an arched gateway, on either side of which lay the single-roomed flatlets always occupied by the leading singers and more illustrious members of the company.

'Does everyone in the company stay here?' she asked as they drew to a stop and people started to alight.

'Mostly. If you're really famous you might get to stay in Mr. Sanderson's own house. But that's only reserved for the high and mighty. Sutherland and Tebaldi, of course. This year you'll have a chance to meet some of the top names from La Scala. They're bound to be personal house guests.'

'That doesn't mean I'll see them,' Sharon said with a wry smile. 'Mr. Sanderson has been away ever since I arrived and I'm not sure whether Maggie and I eat in the nursery when he has visitors.'

'Maggie's father treats her as if she's grown up,' the pianist replied. 'I would be surprised if she let herself be stuck in the nursery. Last year she came to quite a few of the operas and was always at rehearsals. She even criticised the costumes, for *Aida*—said they were too Greek and should have been Egyptian.'

Sharon laughed. 'She's uncannily knowledgeable about fashion. I've never known a child like her.'

'There's only one Maggie,' came the reply, 'and thank goodness for small mercies!' A blunt-fingered hand was held out. 'My name is Gladys Pugh; what's yours?'

'Sharon Lane.' They shook hands and the woman moved off with the rest of the party.

Maggie skipped over to her. 'Isn't it fun now that people are starting to arrive? There are lots more to come. Rehearsals begin on Monday.'

'Will your father be back by then?'

'Daddy will be home tonight. I had a postcard from him.'

Sharon felt a surge of nervousness and anticipation. She was glad she had had the opportunity of settling down at Pailings without Paul Sanderson's eagle eye on her, but would have been reluctant to have remained here much longer without being able to talk things over with him. There were many aspects about Maggie's régime that she did not like, and though he had given her a free rein to do as she wished in this respect, she was reluctant to make any drastic changes in case he had not really meant what he had said.

'Is there a short cut from here back to the house?' she asked her charge.

'We can go through the Elizabethan garden. That will bring us out near the terrace.'

Maggie raced ahead and Sharon followed more slowly, admiring the carefully tended flower beds which were already showing their promise of beautiful things to come, across a hundred yards of springy turf to a large, formally laid out garden. This must be the one to which Maggie had referred. Clipped box hedges enclosed the area and symmetrical flower beds ranged either side of a very narrow path that cut through the centre. There were many flowers and bushes here which Sharon did not recognise, though their scent was so beautiful that she stopped occasionally to sniff at them.

'Daddy designed this garden,' Maggie said, running back to see why Sharon was taking so long. 'There are some flowers here that haven't grown in gardens for hundreds of years. Daddy went to the British Museum to find out.'

'I didn't know your father was a gardener.'

'He isn't,' Maggie giggled. 'But when he makes up his mind to do something, it has to be right.'

Somehow it seemed typical of the man and fitted in with the elegant and precise decor of his home. Attention to detail seemed to be part of his character, and she could imagine him poring over old manuscripts and drawings in order to ensure that his Elizabethan garden was all it should be.

Aware of Maggie waiting for her, she quickened her pace, running the last few yards down the narrow path and through the wooden gate into the garden of Pailings itself. The vast sloping lawns stretched ahead of her, with fields in the far distance and cattle grazing on them. It was a scene of such rural splendour that it was hard to believe it was twentieth-century England, with overcrowding an approaching nightmare. Money could still buy tranquillity, she mused, and knew that her employer must have a great deal in order to maintain this particular life-style.

Maggie was too anxious to start cutting out one of her dresses to eat much lunch, and they were soon kneeling on the floor in the small sitting room, with the paper pattern and fabric spread out around them. Maggie cut the material with the deftness of a girl twice her age, and had no difficulty in following the instructions, though Sharon guessed she was doing it by instinct rather than an ability to read what was written. Soon they were both busy tacking, so engrossed in their task that neither of them were aware of the door opening and the tall, quiet-faced man watching them, until he closed the latch with a snap and came further into the room. Only then did Maggie look up, give a shrill cry of pleasure as she saw her father, and fling herself into his arms.

'Hello, poppet,' he greeted her, and hugged her tight, then set her down and smiled at Sharon. 'I can see there's no need to ask how *you* are, Miss Lane. You both looked so happy I almost decided not to disturb you.'

'I'm making a dress,' Maggie interrupted. 'I went with Sharon to buy the material and the pattern and we're cutting it out. I have a lot more material too—enough for three dresses.'

'I thought you didn't like dresses,' he commented.

'I like the ones *I'm* going to make,' his daughter said, 'but I hate the ones that——'

'What about clearing up the pins, Maggie?' Sharon interrupted hastily.

Obediently Maggie bent to the carpet, and over her curved figure Sharon looked at Paul Sanderson. Her imagination had not played her false. He was as striking looking as she had remembered; better in fact, for he was wearing tweeds in some light flecked material that made him seem younger than at their first meeting. His hair was faintly untidy as though he had been driving an open car, and though it was brushed straight back from his forehead it had a strong natural wave in the front which made one lock stand free of the rest and fall slightly forward, so that he frequently put up his hand to push it back again. She had forgotten how light grey his eyes were, lighter even than Maggie's, with a coolness in them which she thought could quickly turn to ice if he was displeased. Despite his quiet air of calm, she sensed he was not a man to be toyed with. He was used to being obeyed and would brook no argument. Obviously he was in sole charge here and, having seen the vast complex of buildings, she could appreciate the immensity of his task. There were so many other questions she would like to ask Gladys Pugh; not only about the company but about the man to whom it belonged; the man who was standing in front of her watching her with a slightly distant expression.

'I hope you've settled down happily, Miss Lane?'

His question brought her mind back to the present, and she nodded and hastily said she had settled down very well.

'I don't anticipate I will be away much for the next few months,' he continued, 'so if you should need me at any time. . . .'

'There are one or two things I would like to discuss with you now,' she said quickly.

'Later, please. At the moment I'm rather busy. In fact the next few weeks are going to be hectic. Things always are when rehearsals start. It takes time for people to settle down, and it isn't just the cymbals that clash, it's the temperaments too!'

She smiled. 'I saw some of the arrivals today, but they all looked very equable.'

'You were seeing some of the backroom boys,' he said drily. 'The regulars who keep the company going. They aren't the ones with the temperament. Wait until the solo singers arrive, then you'll see some fireworks.'

'You seem to have managed so far without being singed!'

'I'm armour-plated,' he replied. 'One needs to be in the opera world. Singers can be impossibly difficult.'

'You chose opera as a hobby,' she reminded him.

'It's much more than a hobby now,' he said with a faint sigh. 'It's almost a life's work.'

'I'm sure you wouldn't do it if you didn't like it.'

'Sometimes it's impossible to stop. You go on because you're caught up in the very system you created. Each year I keep telling myself I'll hand the whole thing over to someone else.'

'And leave Pailings?'

'Not that,' he said. 'But cut the house off from the company. It's quite possible to do so.'

'Daddy is always saying that,' his daughter interrupted, closing the pin box and jumping to her feet. 'I've tidied the carpet, Sharon. Can we get out the sewing machine?'

'You must finish the tacking first. Now that your father is back, I suggest we do it in the nursery.'

'I want to stay here.'

'There's no reason why you can't,' Paul Sanderson intervened, smiling first at his daughter and then at Sharon. 'You won't be in my way. If I work in the house, I'm generally in the library.'

'You never work in the house, Daddy. You're always in the annexe with the company.'

'Don't contradict your father, Maggie,' Sharon said gently.

'But he's telling lies.'

'He's being polite,' Sharon said calmly, 'and you shouldn't make comments about people in front of them. It's rude.'

'It's rude to talk about people behind their backs,' Maggie retorted.

Her father chuckled and Sharon, conscious of getting the worst of the argument, changed the subject.

'If we're going to stay down here, let's finish tacking your dress so you can try it on.'

Obediently Maggie dropped to the floor and spread out various pieces of fabric around her. She was immediately engrossed in what she was doing and for a long moment Sharon studied the downbent head, its mousey hair pulled back into a pathetic-looking ponytail.

'You've quickly found the way to my daughter's heart,' Paul Sanderson murmured.

'It wasn't difficult to do. She is a lonely child, and she just wants a lot of attention.'

'Don't we all?' he sighed, and turned to the door. He had his hand on the knob when Sharon took a pace towards him.

'About tonight, Mr. Sanderson. I understand from Maggie that you allow her to stay up and dine with you each evening?'

'Yes, I do.' His eyes were watchful. 'Do you object to that?'

'I'm not sure. It depends what time you have dinner.'

'Generally at eight.'

'Don't you think that's rather late for your daughter?'

'She's never complained.'

'She wouldn't. Surely you know all children love to stay up as late as they can?'

'What's wrong if she does? After all, it's the school holidays.'

'I just thought it might be better if Maggie and I ate together at seven. Anyway, this week we've been having our main meal during the day and something light in the evening. I think it's far more suitable for her.'

'Maggie is eight,' he said irritably. 'She doesn't need to eat slops in the nursery. I really see no objection to her dining with me. She enjoys my company, and frankly, I enjoy hers.'

Feeling she had been put in her place, Sharon turned

away. When she looked around again Paul Sanderson had gone, but his presence remained disturbingly close and it was an effort for her to concentrate on his daughter. No wonder Maggie was obstinate and autocratic; she had an autocratic and obstinate father on whom to model herself.

CHAPTER SIX

SHARON dressed for dinner with great care, and was feeling pleased with her appearance when she went along the corridor to collect Maggie. The room was empty, and surmising that she had gone downstairs to her father, Sharon followed.

Voices came from the drawing room and she hesitated for a moment on the threshold. Paul Sanderson was standing by the piano talking to Honor Macklin, and Sharon's pleasure in her own appearance vanished like a stone into a well as she took in the svelte American. Her tall slimness was swathed in an exotically patterned chiffon, with a high neckline and dramatic floating sleeves. Her hair looked even more silver blonde than when Sharon had first seen it and was braided into a coronet on top of her head. Diamonds glittered round the thin throat, their hard brilliance echoed by the look in the eyes which raked Sharon from head to toe.

'A drink, Miss Lane?' Paul Sanderson enquired.

'Sherry, please.' Sharon did not like sherry, but it was the first word that came into her mind and she took the drink he poured for her.

'Where is Maggie?' he questioned.

'I thought she was down here. I went to her room to fetch her, but it was empty. I'll go and see what's happened to her.'

As she turned to do so, the little girl came in. Sharon bit back a gasp. Maggie was wearing the ruby velvet dress from which Sharon had earlier unpicked the lace trimming.

But the child had altered it even further by removing the lace collar and cuffs, leaving a starkly simple dress that bore no relation to the decorative affair it had originally been.

'What on earth have you done to that dress?' Honor Macklin's voice was high with anger. 'You've unpicked the lace!'

'Sharon did it.'

'Really, Miss Lane!' Dark brown eyes flashed, but before Honor could continue, Maggie rushed in.

'I asked Sharon to do it. I wouldn't wear it the way it was. It was hateful!'

'It was a beautiful dress,' Honor was tight-lipped. 'It cost a fortune.'

'I don't care what it cost,' Maggie answered back. 'I wouldn't ever wear it with all that lace. I told you so when you bought it for me.'

'I've never known a more ungrateful child. Here you are, getting the most expensive clothes and——'

'Children aren't concerned with what a dress costs, Mrs. Macklin,' Sharon put in quickly, 'and Maggie felt the dress would suit her better without the trimming.'

'You've allowed her to ruin it!'

'She is at least wearing it, which she wouldn't have done before.'

'You are being insolent, Miss Lane.'

'I only——'

'I suggest we drop the subject,' Paul Sanderson interceded coldly, and the two women lapsed at once into silence, though the look Honor Macklin flashed at Sharon spoke volumes.

With a shaky hand Sharon picked up her glass of sherry. She could understand why the woman was annoyed, and wished she had had the forethought to tell Maggie not to wear the dress when she was there. There was no doubt Mrs. Macklin believed it had been done deliberately to annoy her. Certainly Paul Sanderson thought so, for she felt his eyes regarding her with ill-concealed temper. But it was not discernible in his voice as he resumed his conversation with his guest, and she was glad he made no attempt to draw her into it, for it required all her presence of mind to retain the little composure she had without being called on to make small-talk. But gradually her interest was aroused by what she was hearing, for the discussion had turned to opera, and her employer was speaking of the singers he had booked to appear during the coming season.

'There are still some doubts about Terrazini singing Queen of the Night,' he said. 'Her husband doesn't want her to take any engagements until after the baby is born. It's a question of whose will is stronger.'

'Terrazini, I would have thought,' Honor Macklin said promptly. 'She is the most ambitious woman I've ever met.'

'Career women are,' he replied.

'Men can be equally ambitious,' Sharon said before she could stop herself, and felt her cheeks grow hot as pale grey eyes surveyed her.

'Ambition is less disturbing in a man,' he replied.

'That's a very prejudiced remark.'

'I never said I wasn't.'

Sharon went redder and the American woman chuckled at her discomfiture. 'Really, Paul, don't tease the poor girl. Can't you see you're embarrassing her?'

'It would take more than an expression of my sentiments to embarrass Miss Lane,' Paul Sanderson said, his gaze still on her. 'If you're going to stay here for the summer, you might as well know that I *do* have my prejudices, and one of them—though it may seem regrettable to you—is a dislike of women who put their career before their home and family. I believe one's husband and children have priority over everything else.'

'Are you saying that a woman who wants to get married should never have a career?'

He shrugged. 'You could put it that way.'

'What happens if she can't help herself? Sometimes a talent can't be denied.'

'I have yet to meet a woman with that kind of talent.

70

Men have had it, but what woman can you name?'

Sharon caught her lower lip between her teeth. The question foxed her and she searched for another line of defence. 'It's only in the last fifty odd years that women have been sufficiently emancipated to have a life of their own, let alone the chance of utilising their talent. Until the early part of the century they were regarded as chattels. But if you were to ask the same question a hundred years from now I'm sure there'd be plenty of women one could name.'

'Your answer fails to convince me, Miss Lane. If we consider a great talent to be akin to genius, then it is something that people are born with, and all I'm saying is that women don't appear to have been born with it as many times as men!'

'What about Madame Curie or the Brontës, or Jane Austen?'

'They were all women of talent,' he conceded, 'but not genius.'

'Admit that Paul is right,' Honor Macklin said smoothly, and went to stand beside him. They made a striking couple: both tall and slim, his grey-flecked head topping her silver blonde one by several inches. 'One shouldn't argue with Paul, Miss Lane. He was chairman of the Debating Society at Oxford.'

'It would take more than that information to stop Miss Lane from arguing with me!' Paul Sanderson's earlier irritation had vanished and he was in excellent spirits. 'Anyway, it does do me good to have someone disagreeing with me. One gets tired of having yes-men around.'

'I must remember that.' Honor Macklin threw him an arch look and linked her arm through his as Goodwin came in to say that dinner was served.

For the first time they dined in the large dining room. Only one end of the table was set and it was lit by candlelight, which left most of the room in darkness.

Determined to maintain the precarious peace between the American and her charge, Sharon kept Maggie by her side, but she need not have bothered to do so, for the child was tired and, as the meal progressed, found it difficult to keep awake. Sharon's annoyance with her employer grew. He should never have allowed his daughter to remain up so late. The child should have been in bed long since, not sitting here stuffing herself with pâté and duck at nine o'clock in the evening. She glanced at the head of the table and saw grey eyes resting on her. There was a sardonic gleam in them and she had the distinct impression that he was aware of what she was thinking. His next gesture proved it, for he glanced at his daughter and motioned her to come over to him.

Maggie pushed back the heavy dining room chair and went to his side, nestling herself against him.

'You haven't touched your food,' he said quietly.

'I'm not hungry.'

'I can see that, darling, and I think it would be a good idea if you went to bed.'

'You said I could stay up with you.'

'You've already stayed up with me, and I'll be home for a long time yet. Be a good girl and take yourself off.'

'Can Sharon come with me?'

'Miss Lane is having dinner with us. I'm sure you're big enough now to go to bed on your own.'

Afterwards there was no doubt in Sharon's mind that Maggie would have obeyed her father's request without any further argument, but unfortunately Honor Macklin chose that moment to interfere, setting her fork down on her plate and saying sharply:

'For heaven's sake, Margaret, do as your father tells you and stop acting like a baby!'

'I'm not a baby!' Maggie shouted, and burst into tears, immediately disproving the statement.

'You're overtired, Maggie,' her father said, till keeping his voice gentle. 'Do as Honor says and go to bed.'

'I won't listen to her! I'm your daughter, not hers. She's an interfering old busybody!'

In one swift movement Sharon was by Maggie's side. But her employer was even quicker, for before Maggie could utter another word he picked her up and carried her out. And about time too, Sharon thought mutinously. If he had taken command of the situation a long time ago, Maggie would not be so impossibly spoiled, and visitors would also have been warned not to interfere with her upbringing.

At a discreet distance she followed him, and not until they reached Maggie's bedroom did he set the little girl on her feet. She was crying hysterically and he eyed her half in concern and half in exasperation.

'Leave her to me,' Sharon mouthed, and with a deep sigh he went out.

It took a while for the child to be quietened, and though she eventually conceded that her father had not been unjust in making her go to bed, nothing would make her admit she had been rude to Mrs. Macklin.

'She *is* an interfering old busybody,' Maggie repeated mutinously. 'I won't let her tell me what to do. She isn't my mother.'

'If you'd listened to your father in the first place, Mrs. Macklin *wouldn't* have told you what to do. But when you persisted in behaving in such a silly fashion. . . .'

'I *was* going to bed,' the little girl said.

'I'm sure you were.' Sharon was leaning on the dressing table watching as Maggie ran a brush through her long, fine hair. Worn loose round her face it made it look less peaky and softened the sharpish features.

'Why don't you wear your hair loose with a ribbon?' Sharon suggested. 'It's much prettier than tying it back the way you do.'

'Honor wanted me to wear it loose.'

'So you cut off your nose to spite your face?'

'What do you mean?'

'Never mind.' There were times when it was better to be diplomatic. 'I'll explain another time. Now into bed, me ole darlin', I want to finish my dinner.'

'It will have been taken away by now,' Maggie said heartlessly. 'You'll have to go to bed hungry.'

'I can always raid the larder and have a midnight feast.'

Maggie looked so delighted at the prospect that Sharon immediately regretted her words.

'Let's do that tonight,' the child squealed, bouncing up and down on the bed. Her face was still flushed from weeping, but there was no sign of it in her manner. How like puppies children were, Sharon thought, barking and snarling one minute and then full of high spirits the next.

'We'll do no such thing,' she retorted. 'Now into bed with you!'

Leaving Maggie tucked up for the night, she went downstairs. As the child had predicted, the dining room table was cleared, and voices from the drawing room told her that her employer and his guest were at the coffee stage. Reluctant to disturb them—she was not even sure they had expected her to come down—she went to her bedroom. She was not hungry, but by no stretch of the imagination could she call herself full. She rummaged in her handbag and found a half eaten bar of chocolate, a legacy of their morning out. After she had eaten it she still felt hungry and decided to have a bath. A long soak in hot water would tire her and take the final edge off her appetite; it was the next best thing short of a sleeping pill.

She was not sure what time it was when she awoke. All she knew was that the house was silent and no light from the corridor came through the crack under her bedroom door. She turned over and tried to fall asleep again, but she was too wide awake and, after tossing and turning restlessly, she switched on the light. It was one o'clock. Reaching out for a book, she began to read it. The pangs of hunger, which she realised now must have been the cause of her awakening, were gnawing at her in a way that could not be denied and, after trying to fight them off, she admitted that the only way of getting any further sleep that night was to get herself something to eat.

In dressing gown and slippers she tiptoed along the corridor towards the kitchen. The house seemed unusually large now that it was lit only by the moonlight seeping in through the mullioned windows, but when she put the lights

74

on in the kitchen everything looked so luminescent that her apprehension of a moment ago vanished and she set about finding herself some food. The larder was the best stocked she had ever seen, as was the vast American refrigerator which took up one side of the kitchen wall. Here she found succulent ham and a large bowl of potato salad, and she liberally helped herself to both. A glass of milk and a thick slice of home-made bread completed the feast, and she carried the dishes over to the dinette and sat down. How much more enjoyable it was to eat here than in the formal dining room under Paul Sanderson's vigilant eyes and Honor Macklin's hard brown ones. If the American woman was going to be a frequent visitor here, she would ask if she and Maggie could have their meals on their own. Surely he would see it would lead to less strained relations between the woman and the child, and not be likely to guess that the request also came from her own desire not to see the American? She speared a potato and munched it. It was a good thing she did not have to worry about her figure, she thought, and tightened the cord of her dressing gown. It was a becoming shade of pink and in a soft wool that draped itself around her. It had been a twenty-first birthday present from her brother and had drawn a laughing protest from Anne, who thought her husband's choice totally unacceptable.

'I knew I shouldn't have let you go out and choose Sharon's present on your own,' she grumbled. 'That's a dressing gown for a granny!'

'It's exactly what I want,' Sharon had protested. 'Travelling round in the winter it can be very cold, and living in digs you need warmth, not glamour.'

'Can't you have both?'

'This has got both. What's sexier than pink wool?'

'I give up!' Anne had flung her hands in the air. 'You love it because Tim bought it for you. What a loyal sister you are!'

Smiling at the memory, Sharon speared another potato and washed it down with some milk. She was setting the glass on the saucer when a patter of steps made her hair crawl on her scalp. Motionless, she waited. The steps came nearer and the door inched open to disclose a small, pyjama-clad figure.

'Maggie Sanderson,' Sharon said in her sternest voice. 'What do you think you're doing down here at this time of night?'

For an instant Maggie looked dumbstruck. Then she burst into laughter and skipped forward. 'I'm going to do what you're doing!' she cried. 'I'm going to have a midnight feast.' She put her finger in her mouth and began to whoop like an Indian. 'A midnight feast in a wigwam! Let's eat under the table.'

'You aren't going to eat at all,' Sharon protested half-heartedly. 'You go back to bed this minute.'

Knowing the words were merely lip service to convention, Maggie ignored them and opening the refrigerator, helped herself to a gherkin.

'Where did you find that?' Sharon asked with interest, and was immediately handed one to munch for herself. 'Very well,' she said resignedly. 'Get yourself a plate and I'll cut you some ham.'

'I only want biscuits and milk,' Maggie replied and, getting what she wanted, came to sit at the table. The two of them chewed in companionable silence. 'I'm glad you're looking after me,' she commented suddenly. 'You're much nicer than anyone else I've ever had.'

'I'm glad to hear it,' Sharon said truthfully. 'I like looking after you.'

'Are you old enough to be my mother?'

Sharon was taken aback but was careful to hide it. 'A little too young,' she said cautiously. 'Why?'

'Because I wish you *were* my mother. My real one was hateful!'

Sharon was shocked, but Maggie was unaware of it and noisily gulped her milk. 'She never played with me nor talked to me. All she cared about was singing. That was why she ran away. You see, Daddy wouldn't let her sing at

76

Pailings.'

Uncertain whether or not to try and change the subject, Sharon figured it would be better not to do so. It was the first time Maggie had mentioned her mother and instinctively she felt that some inner aggression was being unleashed this way.

'Sometimes I think I hate my mother more than I hate Honor,' Maggie continued. Her voice was so artless that it was hard to credit she understood what she was saying. But this was disproved by the way she suddenly leaned forward and stared into Sharon's face. 'Do you think I'm wicked to say I hate my mother?'

Sharon hesitated. She knew it was extremely important that she answer this question in the right way, but lacking knowledge of child psychology, she was forced to try and hedge. 'Who says it's wicked?'

'Mrs. Goodwin. She says you mustn't hate your parents. She says children must love their mothers and fathers. Do you think so too, Sharon?'

'I don't believe one person can love another person automatically. You love someone because they're good to you; because they look after you or care about you. If you had a puppy, it wouldn't love you if you didn't feed it and take it out for walks. You would have to show that you loved it, and only then would it feel it was your dog and love you back.'

'Do you love your mummy?'

'I did. But she isn't alive any longer.'

'When she was alive did she keep house and look after you?'

'Yes. But she also taught the piano, so we had lots of children coming to the house to learn. I remember sometimes my mother was too busy to take much notice of me, but if I needed her, she was always there.'

'I was brought up by a nanny,' Maggie drained her milk. 'It was the same nanny who brought up my daddy. She would still be here except she got ill.'

For the first time sadness tinged the thin voice and there

was the sheen of tears in the pale grey eyes—Paul Sanderson's eyes, Sharon thought, though his lashes were thicker and longer.

'Well, *I'm* here to look after you now,' she said quickly, 'and if you've finished your milk, I suggest we go upstairs.' Putting out her hand, she caught the small one and drew the child to her feet. Only then did she see the tall thin figure leaning negligently against the door jamb. The blood rushed into her face and her body grew hot with embarrassment. How long had Paul Sanderson been listening to the conversation? His expression gave nothing away and it was difficult to tell exactly what he had overheard.

'We're having a midnight feast, Daddy,' his daughter said conversationally. 'Have you come down to eat too? Sharon can cut you some ham if——'

'I haven't come down at all,' he interrupted. 'I was on my way to bed and decided to make myself a hot drink.'

Sharon became aware that he was still wearing a dinner jacket. Unconsciously her eyes went past his shoulder and, interpreting the look, he half smiled.

'Mrs. Macklin has gone to her room.' He reached down and lifted his daughter into his arms. She gurgled with pleasure and burrowed against him as he turned round and carried her back into the hall and up the stairs.

Sharon remained where she was, anxious to let father and daughter be alone together. She put a pan of milk on the stove, and by the time it was boiling she had set out biscuits and a cup and saucer on a tray. Not sure what drink her employer had been about to make himself, she opted for chocolate, making it to her own taste and hoping it would also be to his. She was carrying the tray into the drawing room when he came down the stairs, stopping in surprise as he saw her.

'For you,' she said. 'I hope you like chocolate?'

'Next best to cocoa!' He followed her into the room. She put the tray on a small table beside him and was half-way to the door when he called her back. 'Unless you're too tired to sit and talk to me?' he added.

'I'm far too wide awake to get to sleep again.' She perched on an armchair, glad he could not hear how fast her heart was beating. She chided herself for being nervous, and forced a slight smile to her lips, refusing to think of her appearance. For the first time she conceded that Anne had been right: glamour was better than serviceability. What lavish negligee would Honor Macklin have sported had she been caught in the kitchen at midnight? Not that one could imagine her doing something as undignified as raiding the larder.

'Were you encouraging my daughter in bad habits to-night or was she encouraging you?' Paul Sanderson asked softly.

Sharon glanced at him from beneath her lashes. Though his voice was expressionless, there was the faintest twinkle in his eyes. 'I'm afraid I'm the one to blame,' she confessed. 'When I put Maggie to bed tonight I blurted out something about a midnight feast, and of course she latched on to it at once.'

'Maggie has a habit of latching on to everything that she shouldn't. It will be a good thing when she goes to boarding school.'

'Do you think so?'

'From your tone of voice, Miss Lane, I gather *you* don't?'

'I'm not sure. Basically I feel children should be brought up by their parents. But in Maggie's case I can see the advantage of sending her away to school. It must be lonely for her here with you away so much.'

'When she was younger my daughter always travelled with me,' he said coldly. 'I wouldn't send her away now if I didn't think it would be better for her. She has become spoiled and uncontrollable and she needs to be with children of her own age.'

'Wouldn't a good day school be better?'

'She would still look to me for authority, and I'm afraid I tend to spoil her.'

'I can understand why,' Sharon said sympathetically.

'She has no mother and——'

'She's better off without a mother,' he retorted.

Sharon was shocked by his tone, but more so since it was the first time he had shown any emotion.

As though aware of her disturbance he said : 'I'm sorry if you find my remark objectionable, but I prefer to call a spade a spade.'

'So do I,' she said quickly. 'I'm even inclined to call it a bloody shovel!'

He threw back his head and laughed. It made an immense difference to his appearance and took years off his age. He was younger than she had first assumed, she now decided, and wondered if grey hair ran in his family or if it had been caused by his unhappy marriage. Had he still loved his wife when she had left him, or had his love died before they parted? She thrust her hands deep in the pockets of her dressing gown and felt inexplicable reassurance from the warmth of the material.

'You look like a pink rabbit in that get-up,' he said unexpectedly. 'All you need are long white ears!'

She chuckled. 'I can remember having better compliments in my time.'

'I think rabbits are delightful,' he said solemnly. 'All soft and cuddly.'

'But they must be handled with care. Never lift them except by their ears and support them under the haunches.' She jumped to her feet. 'It's getting late. I must be off to bed.'

'I hope I haven't frightened you away? I can assure you I have no intention of picking *you* up by your ears!'

Aware that she had immediately played into his hands, she sat down again. 'I'm not in the least frightened of you, Mr. Sanderson. I just don't want you to think I'm forcing myself upon you the way your other employees did.'

'I can assure you I do not equate you with any of Maggie's erstwhile companions. Anyway, on your own admission, you're tone deaf. So even if you seduced me into a stupor I wouldn't be able to put up your name in lights!'

'I'm not really tone deaf,' she said hastily, unwilling to allow such a blatant lie to stand.

'But you said you didn't sing a note?' His eyes narrowed. 'I take it that's true?'

'Oh yes. I wouldn't sing if you paid me.'

'Excellent.'

Telling herself she was merely stating the truth—albeit in terms that were misleading—she stifled a pang of conscience and looked forward to the time when she could be honest with him. But first he must get to know her. Only then could she risk telling him the truth, for only then would he believe she had not come here to further her own career but because—even though she could not sing for six months—she wanted to work in an atmosphere of music.

'I am glad Maggie likes you, Miss Lane.' His change of subject, though unexpected, was welcome, and reminded her of the many things she had planned to ask him.

'How much authority do I have over her?' she asked. 'You said I had control, but I wasn't sure if you meant it.'

'I never say what I don't mean. You have complete control over her within reason.'

'Within what reason?'

He pursed his lips. 'Well, I wouldn't tolerate corporal punishment, nor would I want you to undermine my own authority with her.'

'What authority?' she asked bluntly.

There was a sharp silence, broken only as he expelled his breath. 'Point taken, Miss Lane. I had a feeling you were going to refer to what happened at dinner tonight.'

'Did you?'

'Yes. You have a very expressive face and earlier this evening you looked as though you wanted to hit me.'

'Not hit you, Mr. Sanderson,' she said with asperity. 'But pick you up and shake you by the ears!'

For a split second he looked dumbstruck; then humour curved his mouth. 'If you ever do that, Miss Lane, I hope you will remember to support *me* under the haunches!'

Sharon's own asperity dissolved and she could not restrain a chuckle at the mental image his words evoked. For the first time since she had met him she felt at ease with him. He had loosened the top of his shirt and undone his black bow tie. It gave him a dishevelled look which made him look disarmingly attractive.

'I find it difficult to lay down the law with Maggie.' He was serious again. 'I feel very conscious that she only has one parent and I suppose that's why I'm inclined to spoil her. Mind you, I don't thing it's such a bad thing. For the first few years of her life she was totally ignored. At the time I never realised it, and ... well, now I'm trying to make it up to her.'

'You'll make her future very difficult if you go on doing it.'

'Really?' His voice was cool again, as if he resented her continuing criticism.

'Yes,' she persisted. 'If you send her to boarding school, the other girls will make her life a misery if she behaves there the way that she does here. She's too spoiled and wilful.'

'That's exactly why I'm sending her away to school.'

'But you aren't preparing her for it.'

'What do you suggest I do? Adopt boarding school rules *here*?'

'At least you should be a little stricter; make her aware that certain things have to be changed.'

'What things?'

'Her bedtime, for example. She shouldn't be allowed to stay up and have dinner with you. Once a week perhaps, or if there's anyone special you want her to meet. But as a general rule she should have a light supper and be in bed by eight, with lights out by eight-thirty.'

'Anything else?'

'She shouldn't be allowed to choose what she wants to eat. She must learn to eat what she is given. Before I came here she seemed to exist on chocolate biscuits, icecream and fruit. And she must also learn to be polite.'

The man gave a snort. 'You'll be a miracle worker if you can do *that*. Politeness has never been one of Maggie's characteristics.'

'Because you encourage her to be rude.'

'That's what Honor says.'

'Mrs. Macklin is right.' It irritated Sharon to admit this, but since she was being honest, she had to be completely so. 'Maggie may not like—may not like certain people, but that doesn't excuse her to go around telling them so.'

'If you can persuade my daughter to show even a modicum of politeness to Mrs. Macklin, you'll have my grateful appreciation.'

'I would prefer to have your authority to put all my other suggestions into operation,' she retorted.

He sighed ruefully and then nodded. 'But I reserve the right to change my mind if I feel Maggie is unhappy.'

'I have no intention of making her unhappy. She may be a bit put out for a few days at having to do as she's told, but I'm sure she'll soon learn to give in. Providing *you* don't give in first.' Sharon stood up. 'I like Maggie, Mr. Sanderson, I wouldn't do anything to hurt her.'

'I'm sure you wouldn't,' he replied, and held open the door for her to precede him into the hall. 'Goodnight,' he called to her retreating back, 'and may the best female win.'

'Not the best,' she retorted over her shoulder. 'But the strongest willed!'

CHAPTER SEVEN

WITH the return of Paul Sanderson, the tempo of the house subtly changed. There were several more additions to the staff, among them his secretary who, during the winter, worked for him in London. There was also an assistant, a young man in his late twenties who spent most of his time telephoning around Europe to make sure that various singers did not get their dates confused and forget to arrive for their engagements, and another man of the same age who was responsible for the general co-ordination of the various sections that went to make up the Pailings Company.

Over all this Paul Sanderson presided with calm control, refusing to let one group believe they were more important than another. There were times when this did not preclude fierce rows from erupting, and Sharon would hear about these during dinner each evening, being careful—whenever her opinion was asked—not to show that she had much knowledge of the way an opera company was run.

True to his word Paul Sanderson was allowing her to make new rules for Maggie's daily routine, and though the child was obstreperous to begin with, she gradually came to accept them. Occasionally she flared into a tantrum at having to go to bed early, but her liking of Sharon was stronger than her dislike of the new régime. Added to this was Maggie's awareness that Honor Macklin disliked both of them, and Sharon wondered what the woman would have said if she had known that part of Maggie's obedience stemmed from the knowledge that by obeying Sharon she was emphasising her refusal to obey Honor Macklin.

April gave way to May. The fine weather broke during the first week and it rained incessantly. Tempers rose and the atmosphere was rife with tantrums as singers, confined to their quarters, worried about the effect of the dampness on their vocal chords. On the seventh day of grey clouds and storms, Paul Sanderson announced he was giving a buffet party for the company. The news immediately decreased the tension, showing clearly how important it was to treat the cast like obstreperous children, chiding them one moment, placating them with a party the next.

The following day caterers arrived from London, bringing a mountain of cutlery, crockery, chairs and tables.

'Why so much?' Sharon questioned Mrs. Goodwin. 'I never thought there were so many people staying in the annexe?'

'There aren't,' Mrs. Goodwin replied. 'But these caterers

run the restaurant during the season, and as they were coming down they decided to bring everything they needed with them.'

'I never knew quite how much work there was behind the whole thing,' Sharon admitted. 'It's like a complete world of its own.'

'It *is* a complete world of its own.' Paul Sanderson had come to stand beside them, and Sharon was intensely conscious of his closeness and wished she was wearing something other than slacks and sweater. But she rarely saw him during the day, and even in the evening he was so preoccupied that she had the feeling he was only half aware of her.

'Things will get even more hectic,' he continued. 'We have another crowd of people arriving this afternoon from the continent. Three Germans, two Italians and a Bulgarian.'

'Not Gregor?' she exclaimed, naming a famous male bass singer.

'You know him?'

She blushed. 'Not know. But I have all his records.'

Dark brows rose above pale grey eyes, and too late Sharon wished she had guarded her tongue. 'I love listening to opera,' she said quickly.

'I'm glad. It would be a pity if you didn't. Living here you will be able to listen to some of the best.'

'When does the season begin?'

'The first week in June.'

'You're lucky the singers arrive so many weeks in advance.'

'They don't all come this early,' he smiled. 'One or two get here with only a week for rehearsal.'

'Those that can spare the time come weeks ahead and look on it as a holiday,' Mrs. Goodwin grunted. 'In the lap of luxury they live, waited on hand and foot!'

'Oh, come, Mrs. Goodwin,' the man smiled. 'Don't you think my singers deserve a bit of cosseting?'

'No, I don't. Nasty, bad-tempered lot they are, screeching and caterwauling into the night! And the fuss they make if anything goes wrong.'

'That's known as artistic temperament,' her employer said equably. 'Talent and temperament go hand in hand.'

'Not so much these days,' Sharon could not help saying, remembering the hard-working singers who had been with her at college. 'Competition is so much keener managers won't put up with temperament.'

'What makes you so knowledgeable on the subject?'

'My brother was a recording engineer with Philips,' she said smoothly, 'and he knew quite a few singers.'

'So that accounts for your interest in opera?'

'I've always been interested in it.'

'Yet you don't sing yourself?' he murmured.

Not waiting for a reply, he moved down the steps and crisply ordered an empty catering van to move along the drive and allow another full one to back into position. Sharon watched him, enjoying the sight of his tall sinewy body as he stepped over to the van and lifted out a gilt chair.

'What do you think of this?' he called to her.

'What should I think? It looks like an ordinary chair.'

'Try it.' He set it on the gravel and she sat down on it.

'Very nice,' she said doubtfully. 'Is there something else about it?'

'It has arms,' he said impatiently.

'So it has.' Immediately she rested her elbows on them. 'Does that make it something special?'

'Of course it does. Most chairs in restaurants don't have arms—which always annoys me intensely. So this year I decided to do something about it.'

She looked at him in admiration. 'And I just thought you ran an opera company!'

He grinned. 'As you said before, this is a world of its own.'

'Don't you ever resent the time you give to it?'

'I love every minute.'

One of the removal men called him and he moved over to

his side, leaving Sharon to rout out Maggie from her bedroom and take her for a walk in the rain. Happily they sauntered along the sodden paths, ending up in a small wooden shelter overlooking the lake.

'Lots of the visitors bring picnics and eat it by the lake,' Maggie confided. 'But I think it's more fun to eat in the restaurant.'

'That's because you are used to all these grounds,' Sharon smiled. 'If you lived in a town all the time you might prefer to eat picnic style too.'

'Mrs. Macklin lives in town, but she hates eating on the grass.'

'Some people do,' Sharon said diplomatically.

'I hope Daddy doesn't marry her,' Maggie continued. 'Mrs. Goodwin says he will.'

'You shouldn't listen to gossip.'

'Mrs. Goodwin wasn't gossiping. She *knows*.'

'No one can know except the two people concerned—your father and Mrs. Macklin.'

'I asked Daddy, but he answered me in a funny way.'

Inexplicably Sharon's pulses raced and she waited expectantly. But Maggie jumped up and raced down to the water's edge, her attention caught by a bedraggled-looking duck. What had Paul Sanderson said in answer to his daughter's question? Had he been evasive or had he admitted he might marry again? It was easy to envisage the svelte American taking charge of Pailings and its master. How well she would fit in with the beautiful surroundings and the glittering life of the opera season. It was not so easy to see her living here in the winter, when the house sank back into itself and the long cold days were empty of visitors. Yet during the winter Paul Sanderson organised the Pailings Touring Company, and he and his wife would surely accompany them for part of the time? Of course he might also spend the winter months in London taking care of his other business interests. Suddenly she wished she knew more about him. It was a pity that conscience wouldn't let her listen to the servants' gossip.

Maggie came back cradling a baby duck. 'It's hurt, Sharon. What can we do with it?'

Sharon looked at the tiny bird which still had its down feathers. 'You shouldn't have taken it away from its mother,' she protested.

'It wasn't with its mother. It was all by itself in the reeds. I think its leg is broken.'

Gingerly Sharon touched it. 'It might be just tired. It's probably been struggling to get free and has exhausted itself.'

'What shall we do with it? If we put it back in the lake it might drown.'

'I've never heard of a duck drowning,' Sharon smiled, then seeing no answering smile on Maggie's sombre face, put her arms around her and gave her a shake. 'We'll take it home and put it in the bath. When it's recovered you can bring it back to the lake.'

At Maggie's insistence they took the duckling into her bathroom, and within a few moments the small creature was floating in the bath like a tiny ball of beige wool. It did not move and Sharon wondered apprehensively whether it was going to die. She racked her brains to try and recall all she knew about ducks, but she had never kept any as a child. She knew about tortoises, rabbits, guinea-pigs and hamsters, but her knowledge of ducks was non-existent.

'I'm sure it will drown,' Maggie cried as the furry body floated to the edge of the bath. 'Please call the vet.'

'I don't think a vet will be able to save it,' Sharon said, getting to her feet. 'But I'll see if I can telephone to one.'

She was half-way across the bedroom when she heard Maggie give a cry, and hurried back to the bathroom to see her bending over the duckling, her pale face wet with tears.

'It's dead, Sharon, it's dead. Look!'

Sharon saw the fluffy body floating on the water, its tiny matchstick legs upturned. Hiding her revulsion, she quickly bent and scooped it up.

'It's all my fault.' Maggie was weeping loudly, as sorrowful as if she had known the duck all of her life. 'It's because I took it out of the lake. I should have left it there.'

'I'm sure it would have died in any case. You said it was caught in the reeds. Don't cry, darling. Let's go down and bury it in the garden.'

'Can we give it a proper funeral with prayers?'

'If that's what you'd like.'

They went down the back stairs and out to the kitchen garden. Sharon placed the duckling on the ground and searched round for a spade. She found one leaning against a wall. It was large and astonishingly heavy, but it was all she could find, and she set about digging a hole. She was just placing the duckling in it when she became aware of a pair of black wellingtons within inches of her nose.

'Digging for treasure, Miss Lane?' a solemn voice asked.

Indignantly she lifted her head and looked into eyes the same grey as the storm clouds around them.

'We're burying a duck,' Maggie said before Sharon could speak. 'It died in the bath.'

With enviable speed of mind, Paul Sanderson followed his daughter's train of thought. 'You shouldn't have brought it into the house.'

'It was injured.'

'And now it's dead,' her father said calmly. 'Are you burying it?'

'Yes. Sharon is going to say a prayer.'

Dark brows rose, but no comment was made, and Sharon bent quickly, put the duck in the hole she had dug and covered it with earth. 'Let's go, Maggie,' she said hastily.

'But the prayer! You promised we would have a proper funeral.'

'Morbid little beast,' her father said affectionately, ruffling her skimpy ponytail. 'I'm sure your duck has gone to heaven without the necessity of a prayer.'

Maggie's mouth trembled and hastily Sharon moved back to the grave. 'Let's pray together quietly,' she said, and knelt down. She was intensely aware of the man watching them, his hands deep in the pockets of his tightly belted mackintosh, his grey-flecked hair glistening with raindrops.

Quickly she mumbled a few words and then jumped to her feet, brushing the damp earth away from her knees. She felt she must look as bedraggled as her charge and she smoothed the fall of hair away from her face, leaving a streaky mark of dirt on her creamy forehead as she did so.

Maggie was still crying. 'I wish it wasn't dead. I've never had a pet before.'

'It was hardly a pet, darling,' Sharon said, cuddling her close. 'If it had lived we would have had to put it back in the lake.'

'Why can't I have a proper pet—one that I can keep?'

Sharon looked over Maggie's head into Paul Sanderson's face.

'Because you're going to boarding school in September,' he replied, 'and there'll be no one here to look after any animal.'

'Goodwin could take care of it. It's very mean of you not to let me have something to love. You're hateful, and it's all Honor's fault!' Maggie tore herself from Sharon's grasp and raced away, a thin, pitiful-looking figure.

Helplessly Sharon stared after her, partly exasperated, partly sympathetic.

'That's the first time I've ever come in for Maggie's favourite adjective,' her father said, looking amused but failing to sound it. 'I never knew she cared that much about having a pet.'

'Do you have any special reason for not letting her have one?' Sharon questioned. 'I mean, if Goodwin wouldn't mind looking after it.'

He shrugged and half turned away from her. His profile was serious and intent, as if his thoughts were unhappy.

'Are you allergic to fur?' she asked suddenly.

'Mink,' he replied. 'Especially when I have to pay for it!'

She was too exasperated to smile. 'You know what I mean.'

'Your question is so pointed, it would be difficult not to.'

'Then what have you got against buying Maggie a dog?'

90

'I offered her a St. Bernard once, but she didn't want it. She said it had to be small so that it could sleep in her room.'

'Most children feel that way. She would probably have liked a big one provided she had a small one too.'

'I don't intend to turn my home into a menagerie.'

'With a couple of dogs?'

'My wife had three yapping poms and I swore I'd never have dogs again.'

Here at last was the real reason for his reluctance to have any animals around him, and with her awareness of it came annoyance. 'Don't you think Maggie's life has already been sufficiently spoiled by her mother without you adding to it?'

'When I want your opinion, Miss Lane, I'll ask for it.' The storm in his eyes was released. 'Don't try my good nature too far. I've already given you a free hand with my daughter, don't attempt to make free with *me*!'

'That's the last thing in the world I'd do,' she snapped. 'And it's a good thing you don't have a dog. You're the sort of man who would kick it!' She swung round to march off, but felt herself caught roughly by the shoulder.

'Kick it, would I?' There was menace in his voice, and as she remained silent he gave her another vicious squeeze and swung her round to face him.

'Kick a dog and kiss an unwilling woman. That's the way you see me, don't you? Well, I won't disappoint you about the second part of your assumption.'

Before she could stop him he caught her head between his hands and covered her mouth with his own. It was a hard kiss and she struggled to free herself from it. But her attempt to do so angered him even more, and his hands left her head and gripped her shoulders, pulling her so close against him that she felt the dampness of his mackintosh through her thin wool sweater. Again she struggled to be free, but he held her as easily as if she were a child and, as if to show his strength, he increased the pressure of his mouth.

Despite herself, her treacherous body responded to his

closeness. She breathed deep of the after-shave lotion he used, coupled with the fragrance of his skin, damp with rain. It was an undefinable masculine scent and she was aroused by it to an extent that frightened her. Never before had she realised a man could awaken her to such passion, and certainly not that it would be her detached and controlled employer. Not that he was detached or controlled at the moment. He was a man of fire and passion; a man too strong to be denied. Accepting this, she relaxed in his hold, and as he felt her tension decrease, the pressure of his mouth lessened.

At once she turned her head away from his. 'Please,' she gasped. 'Let me go.'

The cracked trembling of her voice achieved what her fighting could never have done, for he released her though he still remained close, looking at her with a brooding expression which she did not understand.

'Forgive me, Miss Lane. I didn't mean to frighten you. I should have warned you earlier that when I lose my temper I frequently lose my control.'

'Does loss of control always result in your kissing the nearest woman to hand?' she retorted, drawing back a step.

'Not always. I've just had a flaming row with Caribani,' he named the eighteen-stone mezzo-soprano who had arrived at Pailings yesterday, 'and I can truthfully answer I had no urge to kiss *her*!'

Against her will Sharon giggled. 'She might have found a kiss more effective.'

'Indeed she might,' he agreed, 'but I wouldn't.'

Sharon turned and walked towards the kitchen door, and he fell in step beside her. 'I do mean my apology,' he said. 'And I can promise you it won't happen again.'

'I believe you, Mr. Sanderson.' She turned the door handle and went inside.

He remained on the outside step, and with a slight nod of his head went in the direction of the annexe, leaving her to make her way upstairs, far less in control of herself than she cared to admit.

CHAPTER EIGHT

SHARON felt strangely embarrassed at the thought of seeing Paul Sanderson again and wished she could avoid meeting him at lunchtime. But entering the small dining room, she found the problem solved, for the table was laid only for her and Maggie.

'Mr. Sanderson has been called away,' Goodwin informed her. 'He'll be lunching out.'

'What time does the party begin?' Maggie asked.

'At eight o'clock.'

'Can I stay up for it, Sharon?'

'You can watch some of the guests arrive,' Sharon agreed.

'I stay up the whole time when Daddy gives a party.'

'You may stay downstairs until nine o'clock,' Sharon said quietly.

'What will you do if I don't go to bed?'

'Nothing.'

'Then why should I listen to you?'

'Because I've asked you to, and because you know that what I want is usually good for you.'

'Why is it good for me to go to bed early?'

'Nine o'clock isn't early. At your age I was in bed at eight o'clock every night.'

'Didn't your daddy give parties?'

'Not the same kind as your father. We lived in a much smaller house.'

'I wish I lived in a small house,' Maggie said, chewing thoughtfully at her chicken. 'A small house in a little street, with people living on each side and lots of children to play with.'

'Why don't you invite some of your school friends over?'

' 'Cos they're all soppy and babyish.'

'That's because you're too grown up for your age,' Sharon could not help saying.

'Don't you like me, then?'

Dismayed at being misconstrued, Sharon reached over and tapped the pale cheek. 'Of course I like you, darling. I like you very much indeed.'

Luncheon over, they went to look at the preparations being made for the party. The kitchen was the busiest room in the house, with Mrs. Goodwin chopping away industriously at a mountain of mushrooms and two white-aproned girls preparing pastry. They both greeted Maggie as if they knew her, and Sharon learned that when the opera season began they were in charge of the cold buffet.

'Until a couple of years ago we ran the restaurant, but with food prices the way they are, Mr. Sanderson decided to have something less expensive and more simple.'

'Simple!' Mrs. Goodwin sniffed. 'Three different kinds of cold meat plus chicken and salads, and enough fruit, pie and icecream to sink a battleship!'

'There's never any food left over,' the second girl grinned. 'And we're doubling up on the orders this year.'

'Why is that?' Sharon enquired.

'Because the theatre has been enlarged. Haven't you seen it?'

'I only peeped in and had a glimpse. I'd really like to watch the rehearsals.'

'You must get Mr. Sanderson's permission for that,' Mrs. Goodwin told her. 'Some of the singers object to visitors.'

'I don't think I qualify as a visitor. I almost look upon myself as one of the staff.'

'Staff need Mr. Sanderson's permission too,' Mrs. Goodwin reiterated, and Sharon made a mental note to ask him.

She went into the main dining room and saw that the table had been moved from the centre and was set against one wall. Its shining surface was covered by a crisp white cloth and there were piles of silver cutlery and plates set to one side. Small tables and gilt chairs had already been placed in position, and noting the number of them she realised the party was going to be larger than she had anticipated. But then most of the main company were already in residence, with the last remaining few arriving today. She wondered if Paul Sanderson had gone in to meet the train at Haywards Heath, and then, unwilling to let her thoughts linger on him, went into the drawing room to admire the bouquets of country flowers that decorated it. The Bechstein stood open in the alcove, and she was drawn to it like a bee to a hive. Sitting on the piano stool, she ran her fingers over the keyboard. A ripple of sound echoed in the room and her desire to sing was so strong that it required all her willpower to remain silent. What would happen if the specialist was wrong and six months' silence did not restore her voice to its normal power? The thought was so shattering that she shook as though with fever. Surely the gods could not be so merciless as to give her a beautiful voice and then take it away before she had the chance to use it properly? Had her arduous years of training been for nothing? Yet fate had struck people crueller blows than this, and she remembered many singers who had been cut off in their prime. She at least was alive and well even if she might never be able to sing again. Yet what would her life be like without her voice? She stood up and went over to the window. Her life would go on as it was doing now. She could look after Maggie or little girls like Maggie; or work in an office or store. Yet none of these prospects seemed real to her, and she knew that deep in her heart lay the conviction that in five months' time she would be able to sing again.

Above the patter of the rain which had come down in a fine drizzle all day, and had now increased to a downpour, she heard the hum of a car engine and the grey convertible, its black leather top up against the weather, glided into sight. Paul Sanderson was at the wheel and Sharon stepped hastily away from the window in case he saw her.

She was half-way across the hall, intent on escape, when he came through the front door, and his call made her stop with her hands on the banisters.

'Do you want me?' she asked, trying to look as if she had

urgent business elsewhere.

'If you can spare the time.'

The dryness in his voice told her that he sensed she was trying to avoid him, and she came across the hall and stopped a few feet away from him. Only then did she notice the small wickerwork basket at his feet.

'Where is Maggie?' he enquired.

'In her room. I left her drawing sketches for some clothes. When she shows them to you, try not to be too critical.'

'I'm no judge of dresses,' he commented.

'They're for *Don Giovanni*. Maggie thinks she can improve on the costumes you already have.'

His mouth twitched. 'Don't tell me you're encouraging her to be a dress designer?'

'She has an uncanny flair for it,' Sharon said with conviction.

The humour left his face as he saw she was being serious.

'I mean it, Mr. Sanderson. Maggie is extraordinarily talented for such a young child.'

'Perhaps this will encourage her to go back to being a little girl,' he said, pointing to the basket at his feet.

Instantly she became aware of the snuffling sound emerging through the wickerwork. Astonishment held her motionless, then with a little cry she knelt down and lifted the lid. A wet black nose was immediately placed in her hand and a long pink tongue wetly licked her fingers.

'You darling!' she cried, and sitting back on her knees, clasped the creamy-coloured puppy in her arms. It wriggled ecstatically and tried to reach up and lick her face. Tilting her head back to avoid its tongue, she saw her employer watching her. 'It's adorable! I never dreamed you'd ... when did you buy it?'

'This afternoon, heaven help me. I'm already beginning to have regrets.'

'Oh, you can't!' The puppy leapt from her arms and was snuffling at Paul Sanderson's feet. Picking it up by the scruff of the neck, he placed it firmly but not unkindly back in the basket and closed the lid.

'Why did you do that?' she asked reproachfully.

'I thought it would be more of a surprise for Maggie to open the basket herself.'

Appreciating the point, Sharon looked at him with shining eyes. 'How kind you are!'

He shrugged and walked up the stairs with the basket. At the top he turned and called her. 'Aren't you coming with me?'

'I thought you would rather give Maggie the dog on your own.'

'It was your idea. I'm sure you would like to see her appreciation of it.'

Quickly she ran up to join him, pleased at his perception, and together they went down the corridor to Maggie's room. She was sitting at a table in the corner, intent on crayoning, and they stood for a moment watching her downbent head and serious profile. She looked a slight little thing to have so much spirit and obstinacy, and Sharon found it difficult to believe that her mother could have left her so callously.

'Maggie,' her father called. 'I have something for you.'

The next few moments were a whirl of happiness as the child ecstatically welcomed her new pet. Girl and puppy gambolled together on the floor, Maggie's high-pitched shrieks of pleasure mingling with excited yelps.

'What will it grow up to be, Daddy?' Maggie asked, scrambling to her feet.

'A dog, I hope!'

'Of course it will be a dog,' she said impatiently. 'But what dog?'

'A labrador.'

'I'm glad it isn't a pom like Mummy used to have.'

Paul Sanderson stiffened, though there was no change in his expression. 'I knew you would prefer to have a dog that you could play with in the garden and take for long walks.'

'I would. I would!' She hugged the animal close. 'What's his name?'

'He's waiting for you to give him one.'

'Can I call him Sharon?'

'Hardly,' he said carefully. 'It's a dog, not a bitch.'

'Miss Williams said Honor was a bitch,' Maggie retorted promptly.

Sharon choked, but recovered quickly. 'Why not call him by the colour of his coat? Honey is a lovely name.'

'He's too sandy to be called Honey.'

'Then call him Sandy.'

Maggie clapped her hands. 'How clever you are! I like the name Sandy.'

As though recognising his new name, the puppy clawed at Maggie's legs and she picked him up and cuddled him.

'You'll find his collar and lead in the basket, and here is a list of instructions telling you how to take care of him.' Paul Sanderson took a typewritten sheet from his pocket. 'I suggest you read it carefully and then go and talk to Mrs. Goodwin. Sandy will need four meals a day to begin with, so you'd better introduce him to the cook!'

'You would have made an excellent diplomat,' Sharon murmured to him, and received an amused glance in return.

'I *am* a diplomat, Miss Lane!'

'Why don't you call her Sharon?' Maggie suggested. 'You call Honor by her name.'

'That's different,' Sharon interposed hurriedly. 'Mrs. Macklin is a friend of the family.'

'So I think are you,' the man said quietly. 'Maggie is right. Sharon it will be, if you don't object?'

'Of course not.'

'Will you call Daddy Paul?' Maggie asked.

'Please do,' he said before Sharon could reply.

'Oh, no,' she protested, 'it doesn't seem right. None of your staff do.'

'You aren't staff.'

In the distance there came the sound of a hooter and he glanced at his watch and frowned. 'The rest of the company have arrived. I had better go and see them settled.'

He strode out, and Sharon was grateful for the reprieve.

Despite his asking her to call him by his first name, she could not do so. His surname set up a barrier between them which she felt was important and necessary. It was far less dangerous to think of him as Mr. Sanderson than Paul.

'Look at Sandy,' Maggie pleaded. 'He can walk on two legs.' She was holding the puppy by the forepaws and he was wobbling on his back legs.

'He's too young for you to start teaching him tricks yet,' Sharon advised. 'The first thing we must do is to get him house-trained. I bet your father forgot to buy him a tray and sand.'

'Perhaps Goodwin can give us some. Let's go and see.'

With Maggie cradling the puppy, they went to the kitchen, where the labrador was greeted with various degrees of pleasure. Mrs. Goodwin looked at it with fear, one of the upstairs maids kissed it as though it were a baby, and Goodwin unexpectedly proved himself extremely knowledgeable on the methods required for daily training.

'You don't want to use a tray for a dog,' he said. 'Teach him straight away to go outside.'

'He might catch cold,' Maggie protested.

'He has a warm fur coat,' the butler replied. 'I suggest you take him for a walk every couple of hours and after every meal; and of course first thing in the morning and last thing at night.'

Maggie looked so apprehensive at all the work involved that Sharon swiftly promised to help her by taking Sandy out for his walk last thing in the evening.

'He must learn to sleep downstairs,' she added. 'We'll put his basket in the gardener's room.'

'Why can't he sleep with me? He's only little and he won't be in the way.'

'He won't always be little, darling, and when he's grown up he won't be happy in the nursery.'

Maggie looked ready to protest, but the puppy suddenly squatted on the floor and made a mess, and in the ensuing commotion, the argument was forgotten.

Later that evening as Sharon was staring at the clothes in

her wardrobe and wishing she had something dramatic to wear for the party tonight, Maggie came in to see her. Surprisingly she was in her pyjamas.

'I won't go downstairs tonight, Sharon. I'll listen to you and go to bed.'

'I said you could stay up until nine. I didn't mean you had to go to bed early.'

'I thought you would like me to.'

Seeing this as Maggie's way of saying thank you for the puppy, Sharon gave her a hug, deciding also to accept the child's sacrifice. 'You needn't switch off the light until nine,' she told her, 'and I'll bring you up some icecream or one of the other sweets.'

'I saw a nice peach gateau in the kitchen,' Maggie informed her, 'with chocolate sauce and nuts.'

'Peach gateau it will be, then.'

'Can I stay up until you get dressed?'

'Of course.' Sharon opened her wardrobe door wider and the two of them surveyed the dresses hanging there.

'I like Honor's clothes,' Maggie confided.

'So do I, but they're very expensive ones.'

'I'll make your clothes for you when I'm grown up.'

'I'll look forward to that.' Sharon took out a long tube of soft blue cashmere, the same colour as her eyes. It was a simple dress and owed its beauty to the way it clung to her figure. In this respect at least she felt she could compete with any other woman, and she stepped into it, zipped it up and tightened the belt round her waist, knowing it looked small enough to be spanned by two hands. Paul's hands....

Quickly she began to brush her hair. It crackled with static electricity and she smoothed it away from her face. It was longer than she normally wore it and the ends curled up slightly, the tips of her hair glinting more reddish gold than the rest of it. She had never known it to look as bright as it did now. With precise movements she darkened her eyebrows and applied mascara to her lashes.

'You look just as pretty without make-up,' Maggie commented.

'But I feel prettier *with* it,' Sharon turned from the dressing table and picked up her evening bag.

'Don't forget my peach gateau,' Maggie warned.

'I won't,' Sharon promised, and went down the stairs.

The drawing room was already half full and she hesitated on the threshold, feeling shy. There was no sign of her employer, but as she looked around the room she noticed him deep in conversation with a middle-aged, angelic-looking plump man. It was the conductor Cabini, whose temper was—if rumour were true—anything but angelic.

Her eyes moved again, pausing as they rested on Mrs. Macklin, svelte as always in black silk jersey and diamonds. Immediately Sharon felt like a country mouse and wished she was not wearing cashmere wool. Then pride came to her aid and she tilted her head and stepped forward. This was a house party, after all, the dress she was wearing was more suited to the occasion than the American's elegant creation that shrieked of Paris. As though aware she was being watched, Honor Macklin glanced over her shoulder, her expression hardening as she saw Sharon approach.

'I hear you persuaded Paul to buy Margaret a dog? Don't you think it was unwise?'

'In what way?'

'Just that she'll miss it when she goes to boarding school.'

'But she'll have something to look forward to when she comes home for the holidays.'

'She has her father to look forward to. I don't think she needs a dog.'

'All children need a pet.'

The brown eyes glittered angrily and Sharon moved out of earshot. There was something about Mrs. Macklin that made her hackles rise; possibly it was the proprietorial way she spoke about Maggie, implying that not only did she have the right to comment on the child's behaviour but also to censor it. Sharon reached the buffet. 'Would you care for a drink, madam?' A waiter was standing behind a display of glasses. 'Champagne, whisky, sherry, gin?'

Smiling, she accepted champagne and then searched for

somewhere quiet where she could sit down and make herself unobtrusive. Noticing a space beyond a tall white urn of flowers, she edged towards it and was almost there when she heard a man murmur her name. She looked up, her glass shaking as she met soulful brown eyes. Tony de Seca. What unkind fate had brought *him* here?

'Sharon!' he exclaimed. 'I couldn't believe it when I saw you come in. I had no idea you were with the opera company.'

'I'm not,' she said quickly. 'I'm here as a—I look after Mr. Sanderson's daughter.'

'You what? Is this some kind of joke? You're a singer, not a nanny!'

She glanced round quickly. 'I can't talk about it here, Tony. I must——'

'Then we'll go somewhere else. There are several rooms here, yes?'

She nodded and, because she had no option, led him through the drawing room to a smaller sitting room beyond. There were people here too, but not so many, and they went to stand in the bay of a window, a little apart from the others, a slim, graceful girl with rippling red gold hair and a handsome, swarthy Italian with a chunky body.

'Now then,' he said. 'Tell me again what you are doing here and why you are not singing.'

Quickly she explained about her voice, glossing over the anguish she had felt when she had believed she might be losing it completely, and concluding with the two most important facts: that she must not sing a note for a further five months, and that her employer must not know she could sing at all.

'But that is nonsense,' the young tenor exploded. 'You have a glorious voice. You should make sure that Mr. Sanderson knows about it. You were the best one in college.'

'He has a phobia about employing singers in his home. He made that quite clear to the agency.'

Tony nodded. 'I remember now. When I was here last

year there was some trouble with one of the child's companions.'

'There's always been trouble with them,' Sharon said drily. 'That's why he made the stipulation he did.'

'My poor angel.' Tony caught her hand and drew it to his lips. 'And because of all the stupid girls in the past, you must be made to suffer now.'

'It's very luxurious suffering!' she joked, pulling her hand away. 'I have a sweet child to look after, a lovely home to live in and glorious music to listen to.' Tony continued to look at her and the fear she had felt at seeing him here intensified. She should have known that things were too good to last. There had to be a serpent in the Garden of Eden.

'Don't look upset, *cara mia*,' the young man murmured. 'I won't give away your secret.'

'Why should you?' she shrugged, hoping she looked more sanguine than she felt. 'After all, it's of no importance to anyone except me.'

'And how important *is* it to you?'

'What do you mean?'

The brown eyes were curious. 'Would you be upset at having to leave here? You said Mr. Sanderson would send you away if he found out you had lied to him?'

'Of course I would be upset,' she retorted. 'This is a good job and I've become fond of the little girl.'

'And the father? Are you fond of him too?'

'Don't be ridiculous, Tony. He's my employer.'

'That wouldn't stop you falling in love with him.'

Her body trembled at Tony's words, but she forced herself to laugh, and hearing the sound, the suspicion left his face.

'I am glad you are not in love with him,' he murmured, 'because I am very jealous of any man you look at.'

'Don't be silly.'

'Is it silly to be in love with you?'

'Please,' she begged, 'don't start that again. I told you last time we met that——'

103

'That was six months ago—before I went back to Italy.'

'I haven't changed my mind.'

'But you aren't in love with anyone else?'

'No, but I'm not in love with you either. I wish you would realise that.' She sighed and looked down at the glass she was holding. For nearly a year she and Tony had studied with the same teacher. To begin with she had liked him very much, finding his flattery amusing and his company gay, but gradually his pursuit of her became too intense, growing into a jealousy that had erupted in furious outbursts of temper when he had seen her display any friendliness towards any of the other students, until finally she had been forced to stop speaking to him.

Since leaving college she had only seen him intermittently, when he had begged her to go out with him for old times' sake. His acceptance of a job in Italy had been a welcome relief to her and she had hoped it would be years before she saw him again. It was unfortunate, to say the least, to find he was now part of the Pailings Opera Company and would be living in close proximity to her throughout the summer.

'I have never stopped loving you,' he muttered. 'I telephoned your brother as soon as I got back to England last week.'

'They never told me.' She had received a letter from Anne only this morning and there had been no mention in it of a call from Tony.

'I didn't leave my name,' he admitted sulkily. 'I had planned on going to your house one weekend.'

'To spy on me, I suppose?' she said tartly, remembering this had been a favourite trick of his.

'Why are you so cruel to me?' he reproached, and caught her hand again.

'I'm not being cruel,' she said, trying to snatch her hand back. 'I'm being realistic. I don't love you, and you'll make yourself unhappy unless you accept that fact.'

'I cannot accept something I do not believe. Give yourself a chance with me. Let me be your friend.'

'It wouldn't work.'

'Why not?' He came closer to her. 'We are both staying here; we will see each other every day. Don't push me out of your life.'

'It would be difficult for me to do that at the moment.' She tried to inject some humour into the scene. 'As you said, we're both staying here and we can't avoid each other.'

'You wouldn't be here if Mr. Sanderson knew you were a singer.'

Sharon caught her breath, knowing Tony too well not to see the threat he was implying. 'Tell him, then,' she shrugged. 'It just means I'll have to get another job.'

His brown eyes were bright with intensity. 'You wouldn't care if you had to leave here?'

'No.'

He went on looking at her, a slight smile playing round his small, full mouth. Over his shoulder she saw Paul Sanderson come into the room, Honor beside him. His voice was deeper than any other in the room and at once Tony heard him and turned his head.

'Let us go and tell him, then,' he said pleasantly, and moved towards him.

'No!' Sharon burst out. 'Don't!'

He stopped, his expression triumphant. 'So you aren't as uncaring about remaining here as you would like me to believe?' he smiled.

'It's a well paid job, and I have the chance to watch the rehearsals and hear the operas.'

'Indeed you have. It is an opportunity no singer would turn down.'

'Then surely you understand why I don't want him to know?'

'Of course I understand. And he needn't know so long as you are nice to me.' He saw her stiffen and shook his head in reproach. 'All I want is to be friends with you. I ask nothing more than that.'

Knowing she was being blackmailed but not knowing how to fight it, Sharon nodded. 'Just friends,' she murmured, and turned away from his smile of triumph to find herself looking directly into Paul Sanderson's eyes.

They regarded her unsmilingly and then shifted to the man at her side. 'Hello, Tony,' he said. 'It didn't take you long to sort out the most attractive girl at Pailings.'

'Instinct,' Tony grinned, his white teeth flashing.

'I had better warn you against our young tenor,' Paul spoke directly to Sharon, a smile on his lips but none in his eyes. 'He has a great reputation for being a breaker of hearts.'

'I've realised that already.' It was an effort for Sharon to keep her voice casual, but she must have succeeded, for the conversation became general and then soon turned to opera.

'I am glad you are staging *Norma*,' Tony said. 'One does not hear it enough these days. Always it is Mozart or Puccini; not that I should complain about that. Without those two gentlemen I would be out of a job!'

'I still think you could extend your range,' Paul commented.

'I have no wish to resume my studies all over again.'

'I thought singers always continued with their teachers.' Honor Macklin had joined them, and linked her arm through that of her host.

'I still use my teacher as a critic,' Tony replied, 'but if I were to take Mr. Sanderson's advice and extend the range of my voice, it would mean a great deal of re-training.'

'It would be worth it,' Sharon could not help saying. 'I always felt your voice had a wider range than. . . .' Too late, she stopped. Paul and Honor were looking at her in surprise.

'Sharon is a keen opera fan and has heard me sing,' Tony said easily. 'It is interesting that those who cannot sing so frequently have an ear for those who can.'

'I didn't even know you liked opera,' Honor said brightly. 'I don't think we ever talked about it.'

'And we have no time to do so now,' Paul interrupted. 'Supper is being served.' He guided Honor in the direction of the dining room and Sharon's arm was taken by Tony proprietorially.

'I thought Mrs. Macklin would have succeeded in capturing him by now,' he whispered. 'Last year the company

106

were laying bets on it.'

'That he would or wouldn't?'

'There was no doubt that he would—no one can escape the lovely Honor when she sets her mind to it—the bet was merely as to the time it would take her.'

'If he loves her he would have married her already,' Sharon could not help saying.

'I don't think he wants to get married again. I probably wouldn't if I had had his bad luck. You know the story, don't you?'

'I know Mrs. Sanderson was a singer.'

'Do you know she left him for a Swedish arms million-aire who promised to build her her own opera house?'

'But she had Pailings.'

'Sanderson wouldn't let her sing here after their daughter was born. He wanted his wife to give up her career and devote herself to him and the child.'

Sharon tried to pretend she was not learning anything new, but she was so disturbed by what Tony had said that she could not hide her dismay. She knew of Paul's dislike of career women but found it incredible that he could have refused to let his wife utilise her talent. The thought of the woman awakened the memory of a tall, flaxen-haired figure whom she had once queued all night to hear sing. For Paul to have expected his wife to live at Pailings and not sing in his theatre was like expecting a painter to stand in front of a bare canvas day after day and forbid him to pick up a paintbrush.

'You see, there is always more to everybody than meets the eye,' Tony said. 'Even Mr. Sanderson is a man with hidden obsessions.'

'What are yours?' she asked coolly.

'You are my only obsession.'

She shivered at the vehemence in his words. As a tenor Tony had a voice of liquid gold, but as a man he had a character of dross.

'Don't look so unhappy, *cara*,' he whispered in her ear. 'The next few months are going to be wonderful for us, I promise you.'

CHAPTER NINE

SHARON tried her best to avoid Tony and, aware of this, he frequently came to the house to search her out. Unfortunately Maggie took a great fancy to him, for he would play with her and the puppy, showing a careless disregard for his immaculately cut clothes as he romped on the lawn or chased child and dog through the trees.

Had Sharon not known him better, she might have decided she had misjudged him, or wonder if he had changed for the better in the six months she had not seen him. But she knew only too well his ability to simulate, and sensed he was merely playing a game in order to try and disarm her. He evidently felt that the best way of ingratiating himself with her was through the child, and to this end he was exerting all his charm. Yet she still remained convinced that when he found himself thwarted, he would revert to the spoilt, bad-tempered young man she knew him to be.

Unfortunately he did not have a part in the first two operas with which Paul was opening the season, so he had plenty of free time. The more she tried to avoid him, the more determinedly he sought her out, until she eventually concluded that avoiding him was antagonising her, and that the best way was to accept his presence and not let him know how much she disliked it.

Yet dislike was the wrong word, for when he wanted to be, he was excellent company, and certainly their love of music gave them a great deal in common. But for a reason which she could not define, his nearness irritated her, and his habit of constantly touching her set her nerves on edge.

'You are always so tense with me,' he commented one afternoon as they strolled in front of the entrance to the theatre. Gardeners were busy on the flower beds that lined this part of the drive, and workmen were repainting a couple of the signs, one of which directed visitors to the buffet and the other to the car park.

'I must be reacting to the mood of Pailings,' she replied. 'Everyone seems to be on edge.'

'It is always like that before the opening night. Once the season is under way, things will settle down.'

'You're lucky to be singing here,' she commented.

'Not lucky,' he protested, flashing her a smile. 'Don't forget that when I met you I wasn't an ordinary student. I had already done my training in Milan. I only came to London because your teacher was so highly recommended.' He caught her hand. 'I am so glad that I did come; otherwise I wouldn't have met you.'

'Don't tell me you've been pining for me since you went back to Italy?' She tried to pull her hand free, but he wouldn't let it go. 'If I hadn't been here looking after Maggie, we would never have met again.'

'I telephoned you the moment I returned to London,' he reminded her reproachfully, 'and you were constantly in my thoughts. Why else would I have gone on writing to you when you never answered any of my letters?'

Sharon bit her lip. It was true he had written to her several times since he had left England and that she had not answered any of his correspondence, hoping that time and circumstance would make him accept that here was one girl who did not respond to his Latin charm. Again she thought how unkind fate was to bring him to Pailings.

'There are other girls who would be delighted by your attention,' she said lightly. 'You would be far better to concentrate on *them*.'

'One cannot direct one's heart. You are adorable, Sharon, and I love you madly. Even more madly when you try to be indifferent to me.'

'I am not *trying* to be indifferent, Tony. I *am*.'

'Now you are being cruel.' He drew her hand to his lips and kissed her fingers.

Angrily she pulled her hand free, but not before Paul Sanderson, coming out of the theatre entrance, saw Tony's flowery gesture. 'The wardrobe mistress is looking for you, Tony,' he said pleasantly. 'You have a costume fitting.'

With profuse apologies for having forgotten, the young Italian hurried away and Sharon watched him go without regret, aware that her employer was doing the same.

'It might be better for you if you didn't encourage Tony,' he said. 'He's here to sing, not to play Romeo to your Juliet.'

Sharon caught her breath in anger at the unjust accusation.

'Tony doesn't need any encouragement from me, Mr. Sanderson, nor is he receiving any.'

'He was kissing your hand.'

'And I was trying to pull it free!'

'You must be giving him some encouragement,' he said flatly. 'I suggest you stay away from this part of the grounds and make it plain he isn't welcome at the house unless he is invited.'

'I've already said that, but he won't listen.'

'Then I'll tell him.'

'No,' she said quickly, afraid that if he did so, Tony might tell him the truth about her.

'Make up your mind,' Paul Sanderson said coldly. 'Either you want Tony hanging around you or you don't. And if you don't, then a word from me is the best way of achieving it.'

'I'm not a child, Mr. Sanderson, I can take care of myself.'

'As you wish,' he said coldly, and strode away.

Perturbed by the sharp exchange that had just taken place between them, Sharon went into the theatre. In the last week Paul Sanderson had been noticeably on edge with her and she had frequently looked up to find him watching her. She had finally become so uncomfortable that she had taken to having her supper on a tray in her bedroom, but two nights ago he had sent a message for her to come down, and on her entry into the dining room had informed her that she was not to hide herself but to help him entertain various singers and members of the company whom he invited to his home each evening.

110

'I hadn't realised that was one of my duties,' she had been provoked to say.

'I was hoping you would consider it a pleasure. Most girls would.'

'Only if they were opera-struck,' she had retorted. 'Personally I find it boring to listen to continuous conversations about music.'

Had she deliberately searched for the most wounding thing to say to him, she could not have succeeded more, for his grey eyes flashed with anger, though he had made no comment.

Today, seeing her with Tony, had been the first exchange of conversation they had had since that night.

It was unnerving to live in a man's home and know he was annoyed with you, and she wondered if this was why she could not get him out of her mind, or whether her awareness of him stemmed from a deeper, more frightening reason. But she refused to analyse it. She was only here on a temporary basis. Four months from now Maggie would be going to boarding school and she would be able to pick up the threads of her career. She thought suddenly of her agent and determined to write and remind him that she was available for work again in the autumn.

Opening the door of the auditorium, she stepped inside. Even empty, the theatre had an atmosphere that was almost tangible, as though the singing and the music and applause still lingered in the air, unheard by the human ear but nonetheless still vibrating. Who was it who had said that sound never died but only became fainter and fainter? Careful not to stumble in the dark, Sharon took a seat a few rows behind the director, who was shouting instructions to a group of people on the stage. There was no scenery on it, merely chairs arranged to signify where the furniture would be placed. Two women and a man were standing together, and Sharon was thrilled to recognise the woman as one of the leading bel-canto singers of the decade. It was obvious that a rehearsal for *Norma* was in progress, and she settled down to enjoy it, marvelling at the amount of detail that was

111

discussed before the scene began. Bar by bar the director examined the aria, uncannily able to show exactly where he wanted inflection put, even though he did it in a voice that would have made a frog blush with shame. The woman at the piano played a chord and Sharon recognised her as the accompanist with whom she had travelled on the charabanc when the first members of the opera company had arrived. It seemed such a long time ago, yet it was not more than a month. If the rest of the time went so quickly, she would be able to start singing again before she had had the chance to miss it too much. On stage the two men moved into position and the pianist played another chord and then went into a melody. Sharon settled back to listen, closing her eyes as the glorious sound washed over her.

'Stop!' the director called in the middle of the aria. 'There is no need to finish it. We will do the second scene of the first act. Elspeth, will you take it from *"E madre sei"*.'

The woman giggled like a schoolgirl, her large bosom heaving. 'How right you are, Tibor.'

'Why? What have I said?'

'I thought you knew?' The woman giggled again. 'It is lucky *Norma* is being performed at the beginning of the season and not the end, otherwise I would be too fat!'

There was general laughter and Sharon joined in. '*E madre sei*'—'You are a mother'—were the words that had given Elspeth Gross the chance she was looking for to tell everyone she was expecting her third baby.

The director was talking to the singer again and she was listening intently, nodding each time he paused and then bending to make a mark in the score she was holding. Once again the pianist started to play and Elspeth Gross began to sing, her voice as clear as a bell. Several times during the next ten minutes she was stopped and corrected. It was more a question of learning stage direction than having to alter her singing, for it seemed that the director wanted to lose some of the static quality of *Norma* and to invest it with more movement.

'If people wish only to hear the opera they can buy the records,' he shouted when Elspeth protested at one piece of stage direction he was giving her. 'I won't have my singers standing like dummies waving their arms. You are a woman in despair and you must act like one.'

'I am a High Priestess,' Elspeth reminded him.

'In this scene you are a mother and you have your children around you. Now let us take it from the top.' He glanced at his music. ' "*Vanne e li cela. . . .*" '

Once more the diva started to sing, and this time she was allowed to go right through the scene without interruption. Listening to the purity of the tone and the careful phrasing, Sharon knew she still had to learn a lot, knew too what a golden opportunity it was for her to sit here and listen.

It was an effort to tear herself away, and only the knowledge that Maggie would be waiting for her for tea made her tiptoe out of the auditorium. Stepping from darkness into light, she bumped into a man standing outside the door. It was Paul Sanderson. Even before she looked up and saw him, she recognised his after-shave lotion.

'You still here?' he said.

'I was listening to *Norma*. It was fascinating, almost like a concert performance.'

'Many people don't like concert performances. They need the panoply of scenery and costumes.'

'I prefer a concert performance. Costumes and scenery often detract from the singing.'

'Why not just listen to the record?'

'Records can be soulless!'

Her answer seemed to please him, for he gave a sudden smile. 'I'll take you to a concert performance of *Norma*. Pailings Opera Company are giving one at the Festival Hall at Christmas.'

'I'll have left Pailings long before then,' she said before she could stop herself.

'That doesn't mean I won't be seeing you.'

She longed to see something deeper in his words, but was afraid to do so. 'You're so busy, you might have forgotten by then.'

'Not so busy that I'll forget a promise.'

'There you are, *cara*!' Tony's mellifluous voice interrupted them as he came striding forward. 'So you were able to wait for me?'

'I wasn't waiting for you,' she said quickly.

'Of course not,' Tony replied in a disbelieving voice. 'No girl ever admits she is waiting for a man. Isn't that right, Mr. Sanderson?'

Paul Sanderson nodded, and Sharon saw that his expression was bleak again. 'Maggie is waiting for you,' he informed her. 'When I left the house she told me to find you.'

'I was just on my way back.'

'Good—you were engaged to look after Maggie.'

Her face flamed. 'Maggie particularly asked to be alone this afternoon.'

'She is making Sharon a birthday present and she wants it to be a surprise.' Aware of Sharon's hurt, Tony came to her defence. His words had the desired effect for Paul looked discomfited.

'I'm sorry, I didn't realise.'

'Why should you?' she said stiltedly. 'Though it would have been nice if you'd given me the benefit of the doubt.'

He did not answer, and slipping between him and Tony, she hurried away.

'*Cara*,' Tony called after her, 'wait for me!'

'Leave me alone!' she cried, and ran even faster.

She was breathless when she reached the house, and she paused in the hall to smooth her dishevelled hair before making her way to the day nursery. Tea was already on the table and Maggie was looking at the cream cake with longing.

'So Daddy found you,' she cried. 'You promised to be back by four.'

'I was listening to a rehearsal and I forgot the time,' Sharon apologised as she helped herself to a sandwich. 'But you shouldn't have sent your father after me.'

'I didn't. He came to have tea with us and when you weren't here he said he would go and find you.' She glanced at the door. 'Didn't you bring him back with you?'

'No. I didn't realise he intended to come.'

'He probably won't now,' Maggie said dejectedly. 'Once he goes over to the theatre he can never escape.'

'That's where you're wrong, poppet,' a deep voice said, and the man they had been talking about came into the nursery. Again there was a change in his mood. He was smiling as if he did not have a care in the world, including Sharon in the warmth of it so that, as always when he was nice to her, she felt an inner glow of happiness.

Careful to hide the inexplicable tremble of her hands, she poured the tea, concentrating hard not to spill any in the saucer.

As though aware of her nervousness, he took the teapot from her. 'Sit down and let me play Daddy.'

'You *are* Daddy,' Maggie laughed.

'So I am, thank you for reminding me!' He finished pouring the tea and then looked with mock horror at the plate of thin sandwiches. 'Is that supposed to be food for a starving man?'

'Mrs. Goodwin didn't know you were coming,' his daughter giggled. 'Sharon can go down and get some more bread and butter.'

'No, no,' he said quickly, as Sharon went to do so. 'I was only teasing. A cup of tea is all I want.' To belie this he helped himself to an éclair and then took a second one.

'It's lucky you don't have to watch your figure, Daddy,' Maggie said.

'Very lucky.'

'Sharon doesn't have to watch hers either!'

'I should think many other people watch it instead,' Paul Sanderson replied, and Sharon blushed at the way he looked at her.

'Tony has to be careful,' Maggie went on. 'He never eats anything when he comes to tea. He won't even have milk.'

Some of the humour left Paul Sanderson's face and,

115

watching him, Sharon could not restrain a tremor of excitement. He was jealous of Tony. There was no other way to interpret his reaction. It also explained his anger this afternoon when Tony had implied that she had only watched the rehearsal while she was waiting for him.

'I didn't know Tony was a frequent visitor here?' Although the question was directed at Maggie, the man's look was directed at Sharon, and she picked up the challenge and answered him.

'I knew Tony in London. I met him at—at a party last year.'

'Is that why you were so anxious to work at Pailings?'

'I had no idea he was singing here. I was astonished to meet him again.'

'Well, he appears to be taking advantage of your presence.'

'Tony can't help flirting. But there's no harm in him.'

Sandy was sniffling at her feet and she bent and picked him up, finding it a release from embarrassment to concentrate on him. He was warm and cuddly and she buried her chin against his fur.

'Your hair is the same colour as Sandy's coat,' Maggie piped up.

'Oh, surely not,' Sharon protested. 'It's much darker.'

'Not where it has caught the light,' Paul Sanderson interposed, his good humour restored. 'You look considerably better since you've been here, Sharon.'

'Because I feel as if I'm not working. Each day is like a holiday.'

'You're the only one of my daughter's companions ever to say that.'

Although he was still smiling, the words reminded her of her position, forcing her to remember that she was not a friend of the family but an employee. 'You haven't been very lucky with your staff, Mr. Sanderson.'

'You aren't staff,' Maggie chipped in, 'you're family.'

Since this was exactly what Sharon did not consider herself to be, she ignored the remark, but she had reckoned

116

without the man, who went on looking at her, his grey eyes as intent as his daughter's.

'Maggie is right. You're one of the family and you can't go on calling me Mr. Sanderson. It makes me feel like Methuselah.'

'Do call Daddy Daddy,' Maggie said, spluttering with excitement.

'Not on your life!' her father retorted. 'I hope Sharon doesn't think me as old as *that*.'

'I don't think you're old at all,' she said coolly.

'Then prove it by calling me Paul.'

Hastily she bent over the puppy, pretending he had attracted her attention. Guilt at the subterfuge that had brought her here made it hard for her to relax. Her desire to tell Paul Sanderson the truth about herself was stronger than it had ever been, and had Maggie not been present, nothing would have kept her silent.

'Where did you go to school, Sharon?' His question was so surprising that she almost dropped the puppy.

'I went to a local one in London.'

'And university?'

'No.'

'Didn't you want to train for a career?'

Reluctant to lie to him totally, she said: 'I wanted to go on the stage.'

'Thank goodness you didn't. I have a profound dislike of actressy women.'

Thinking of the way Honor Macklin postured and posed whenever people were present, she found this hard to accept. Or was he so used to her that he no longer saw her with a clear eye? 'All women are actresses,' she answered lightly. 'They have to be if they're going to deal with men.'

'And what exactly does that mean?'

'Just that men want women to be all things to them.'

He smiled. 'Wife, cook, mother, mistress, good companion. Are you suggesting a woman never has a chance to be herself?'

Sharon considered it more diplomatic to reply with a

117

smile rather than words, and he allowed her to get away with this and turned his attention to his daughter who was clamouring for him to look at some dress designs she had made. He studied them as carefully as if they had been submitted to him by his own costume designer.

'These are very good, poppet,' he said at last. 'Did Sharon help you with them?'

'They're all mine,' Maggie protested. 'I asked Sharon to help me, but she wouldn't.'

'I thought it would be more interesting to see what Maggie could produce on her own,' Sharon explained, and pointed to one of the sketches. It was a full-skirted dress with a bouffant skirt over a contrasting underskirt. Though a dress of the eighteenth century, it had an air of modernity that would have made it suitable to wear today. 'This is Maggie's idea for what Donna Anna should wear,' she said.

'Is it?' Paul Sanderson ran a hand through his hair, dishevelling it. The grey flecks were noticeable and contrasted with his face, which was youthful. 'It would be interesting to bring *Don Giovanni* down to the twentieth century. I don't think anyone has done it as far as I'm aware.'

'I think they have,' she murmured, and mentioned the name of a small opera company in Bavaria, noted for its avant-garde approach.

He flung her a keen glance. 'You're full of surprising snippets of information. Who told you that little bit? Tony?'

She nodded, unwilling to say she had learned it from her teacher. Knowing her silence would make him associate her even more with Tony, she sought for a way of changing the conversation and picked up another of Maggie's sketches. This time it was for Don Giovanni himself, an elegant costume suitable for a dashing lecher. This time the face had also been sketched in: a firm-jawed one with an unmistakable quiff of hair over the forehead and thick eyebrows.

'So this is how my daughter sees me?' he murmured. 'The Don Giovanni of Pailings! Do you see me that way too?' He was openly laughing at Sharon and she relaxed again.

118

'You're far too reserved to be a Casanova. A man who loves women so indiscriminately cannot have any finesse.'

'I'm flattered that you think I have finesse.'

'And pride too.'

'Everyone should have pride. It stiffens the character and gives you the determination to succeed.'

'Pride can also make you rigid.'

He took the sketch from her hand and looked at it for a moment. 'Do you find me rigid, Sharon?' he asked softly.

She nodded and turned away, reluctant to say more in front of Maggie. But the child was playing with the puppy, seemingly oblivious of anything else going on around her.

'You surely don't think I'm too rigid with my daughter? You're always telling me I spoil her.'

'Rigidity implies inability to change!'

His smile was sardonic. 'Now you're playing with words. But then neither of us are saying what we mean.'

'Aren't we?'

'*I* am not. There are many things I haven't yet put into words.'

'You're making me afraid.'

'Never be afraid of me! That's the last thing in the world I want.' He spoke with such vehemence that she could not hide her surprise, and seeing it, he knew he had to explain more. 'If people are afraid of each other they can never achieve any understanding. So much of our life is lived on the surface that we should take every opportunity we can to be close to someone.'

'I'm surprised you feel that way.'

'Do I seem so detached to you, then?'

Sharon hesitated, but decided to be truthful. 'You give the impression of being self-sufficient. As if you have no real need of anybody.'

'I need someone, all right,' he said thickly, 'but I've never had the luck to find the right person.'

'Were you never close to your wife?'

'Never.' His voice was harsh. 'She was the last woman in the world I felt close to.'

'But you married her.'

119

'I'm afraid we all make mistakes at one time or another.'

Out of her depth, she subsided into silence. It had been stupid of her to refer to his past. Yet no matter how much he denigrated his wife, she could not believe he would have married her unless he had been in love. Obviously he was still bitter because of the way she had left him, and this alone indicated how deeply he must feel about it. She longed to hear his side of the story, but knew that now was not the time nor the place to show her curiosity. Even if he did agree to talk of it, he would not do so in front of his daughter, who had now stopped playing with the puppy and was looking at them with curious absorption.

'Will Sharon have to leave here when I go to boarding school?' she asked unexpectedly.

'Your father isn't going to employ me to look after Sandy,' Sharon smiled.

'But you could look after Daddy,' Maggie suggested.

Sharon blushed but ploughed on manfully. 'I think your father is quite capable of looking after himself.'

'Honor doesn't think so. She says he needs a woman to take care of him.'

'Little pitchers have big ears,' her father murmured.

'What does that mean?'

'It means you talk too much, poppet.'

'But I only——'

'Sandy's crying to go out,' Sharon interrupted, scooping the puppy off the floor and dumping him into Maggie's arms. 'Take him downstairs and put him on the lawn. If he's a good boy, don't forget to pat him on the back and tell him so.'

'If he's naughty while I'm holding him, I'll smack him,' Maggie said decidedly, and hurried him away.

Sharon smiled, but alone with Paul Sanderson, felt an unexpected embarrassment.

'What's my first name?' he demanded abruptly.

'Paul,' she said, startled.

'Say it again.'

Conscious of her cheeks growing pink, she did so.

120

'And again,' he ordered.

'No, I won't. You're trying to embarrass me.'

'And succeeding too, if your colour is anything to go by! Actually I'm trying to show you how easy it is to call me by my name. If you can call Tony by his. . . .'

'I don't think of you in the same way.'

'Is that meant as a compliment?'

At this she had to smile, and wished wholeheartedly that she could tell him how much she disliked the Italian. But fear held her silent. She dared not tell her employer the whole truth yet, though there were some things she could clarify.

'I meant what I said to you before about Tony. I had no idea he was singing here, nor do I particularly like him. But I've known him a long time and . . . Well, as you said yourself, he *is* a flirt.'

'So much so that I nearly didn't re-engage him for this season,' Paul Sanderson responded. 'If he makes a nuisance of himself I'll get rid of him, contract or no contract.'

'He isn't difficult to control,' she said hurriedly, unwilling for Tony to be dismissed on her account. 'Please don't think I'm complaining about him.'

'I would feel happier if you did.'

The remark could be taken two ways and she decided to take it at its face value.

'He hasn't done anything for me to complain of.' She walked over to the table and started to gather up the crockery.

'Are you happy here?' he asked behind her.

'Very happy.'

'It can be lonely in the winter.'

'I won't be here in the winter.'

'But if you were,' he persisted, 'wouldn't you find it lonely? The opera house is closed and though we give some concert performances at Christmas and early in the New Year, for the most part the house is empty and we have no visitors.'

'Aren't you away then too?'

'I sometimes go on the road with the touring company. But that's mainly because I don't like staying here by myself.'

Here was her opportunity to ask him what else he did, and she put the question to him lightly.

'I'm an accountant,' he said, 'and I went into property development with one of my clients. It was disgustingly profitable and the only way I could appease my conscience was to use the profit to establish an opera company here.'

'You're lucky you had Pailings. It's an ideal setting.'

'Without Pailings, I wouldn't have had the idea of starting an opera group as a hobby. Now it's more than a hobby —it's a life's work.'

'You sound as if you resent it.'

'In a way I do. Never let yourself be possessed by anything, Sharon. Obsessions can destroy your happiness.'

'What obsessions are you thinking about?' she asked clearly. 'The obsession to pursue your talent—the way your wife did?'

She heard his quick intake of breath and knew she had gone too far.

'Forgive me,' she said quickly. 'I had no right to say that.'

'It doesn't matter.' His voice was jerky, unlike its normal measured tones. 'You're merely stating the general misconception of what happened. I suppose I have only myself to blame for it, but I could never bring myself to set the gossip to rights. Pride again, I suppose, which made me refuse to give an explanation to anyone.'

'You have no need to tell me about it either.' She busied herself with the crockery again, but stopped as she felt his hand on her shoulder.

'You are the one person I'm quite happy to explain it to.' Gently he swung her round to face him. 'My wife was Helga Lindstrom—as you probably know. It's a name that meant a lot to opera-lovers ten years ago.'

'I have heard of her,' Sharon said quickly. 'She had a

122

lovely soprano voice.'

'A great one at the peak of her career,' he corrected. 'It was a feather in my cap when she agreed to come here to sing. I married her before the season was over. I loved her so much I couldn't bear to let her go away.'

Jealousy rasped Sharon like a serrated knife, and she bit her lip hard to stop herself from crying out. Paul was speaking again and she forced herself to concentrate on what he was saying and not to think of the painful truth that was staring her in the face; a truth which, until this moment, she had refused to acknowledge and which she could no longer hide.

'Maggie was born exactly nine months later,' he went on. 'The only saving grace about her as far as Helga was concerned was that she was born at the beginning of the opera season, so that it didn't stop her from singing at Pailings again. You see, singing was all-important to her. More important than anything else. Certainly more important than her child or husband. I considered *such* a desire to sing as an obsession, but you would probably call it a need to exercise one's talent.'

Sharon acknowledged the jibe, feeling guilty that she should deserve it. 'It can be difficult to change one's way of life,' she commented. 'It requires such dedication to be a singer that when you finally get to the top you can't relinquish the position.'

'Don't make excuses for Helga,' he said sharply. 'She wouldn't have thanked you for it.' He frowned. 'Now I've forgotten where I was.'

'Maggie had just been born.'

'Ah yes, and Helga went straight back to singing. But something had gone from her voice. *She* wasn't aware of it, but I was. There was a change in the tone and the power. I thought it was because she was overtired—that the pregnancy had taken more out of her than she realised. So I persuaded her to rest, to come away with me on an extensive tour and not to sing again for several months. She thought I was trying to make her retire and she refused to listen to me.'

'Didn't you get her to see a throat specialist?'

'She saw several, and they all advised her to give her voice a rest. She refused to take any notice of them. She thought they were saying it because I had asked them to—that I had bribed them.'

'She couldn't have thought that! That was crazy.' Sharon stopped. 'I'm sorry, I had no right to say that.'

'Why not? You aren't wrong. Looking back on it I think she *was* crazy. But at the time I didn't see her so clearly.' He sighed deeply. 'During the next season her voice was noticeably worse. Not all the time, but too frequently for it not to be commented on. One of the doctors who had seen her told me he suspected throat cancer and begged me to get her to come and see him again, but when I asked her to do so, she said I was trying to frighten her. The more I denied it, the more she insisted I was lying. Eventually I did the only thing I could. I refused to let her sing at Pailings until she went to see the specialist. In a temper she went to London and got a job with another company. Covent Garden wouldn't take her, but there were several smaller ones only too eager to use her name. I went after her, of course, and begged her to do as I had asked. By then I had seen the specialist for myself, and he was pretty sure she could be cured. She wouldn't have been able to sing again, but she would have lived.'

'What happened?'

'She accused me of being an insane liar,' he said bleakly. 'In order to prove she had no intention of coming back to me again, she gave me evidence for divorce. With one of her compatriots,' he added, 'a Swedish arms manufacturer who decided to build an opera house for her in Stockholm.'

'Didn't he know she was losing her voice?'

'I think his career in firearms had deafened him. He saw her beauty and her body; he wasn't concerned with how good her voice was. I went to see him—I had to make him appreciate how ill she was—but he didn't believe me. A year later, after she had died, he wrote me a letter of apology.'

'That must have done you a lot of good,' Sharon said.

'By that time I didn't care any more. I had faced up to the fact that I'd made a fool of myself over a woman who had never existed outside of my imagination. Helga should never have married. Singing was the only thing she cared about, and she finally let it kill her. That's why I vowed I would never again get involved with a career woman.'

'I can understand how you feel,' Sharon murmured, 'but surely you can't judge all women because of the way one of them behaved?'

'I base my judgement on what happened to me then, and what has happened to me since. In the five years since Helga died, Pailings has become world-famous. There isn't a singer of repute who hasn't appeared here, and there isn't a singer I've met who wouldn't consider the world well lost in order to be able to sing one note higher or one note lower!' He threw out his hands. 'Not that I blame them. To succeed in their profession they need a terrible single-mindedness. It's worse than being a violinist or a pianist. Not only does it require years of physical and mental dedication, but even when they are at the top, they know they can only stay there for a short number of years. And during those short years, nothing and no one is more important than their voice.'

'But singers do relax,' Sharon protested. 'Many of them are happily married with families.'

'The husbands and families must come second.'

'That isn't true.'

'I'm a better judge of the operatic world than you are, my dear.'

'You're biased,' she retorted.

'And you're judging a world you've only seen since you have been living here. Believe me, Sharon, I know what I'm talking about.' The sadness had left his face and he was smiling slightly. 'Don't look upset about it. I was hoping you would be pleased at how I felt.'

125

'Why should I be pleased?'

'Because you have no need to be jealous of all the exotic songbirds who come down here.'

'I would rather be jealous of them than have you believe in a misconception. As I said before, it's wrong to judge all women on the basis of one.'

'Not all women,' he said. 'Only opera singers.'

'Then you should give up opera and go back to accountancy!'

'And fall in love with a clerical assistant?' he chuckled. 'I don't need to do anything as drastic as that. I just avoid romantic attachments with anyone in the company and refuse to get involved with anyone who has operatic ambitions. That still leaves a world of women.'

Sharon knew he was teasing her, but she did not find it amusing. She was a singer too, one of the band of women he had denigrated. 'You might fall in love with a singer,' she ventured. 'Some of them are very beautiful, and you can't always dictate to your heart.'

'I can. *I have.*'

'How sure you are!'

'More sure now than I've ever been.'

'What would you say if I told you *I* was a singer?'

The humour left his face and his eyes became a deeper grey as he relived the dark memories of the past. 'But you aren't a singer, Sharon. If you were, you wouldn't be looking after Maggie.'

'I could have come here under false pretences.' The truth was urging to be told and she was searching for a way of doing it.

'You could never pretend, Sharon. The thing I first liked about you was your honesty; the way you said what was in your mind without fear or favour.'

The fear that she would lose his favour if he knew she had been lying kept her silent. Now was not the time to tell him the truth. It would be better to do so when the memory of Helga was not so clear in his mind. He had accused his wife of being blindly prejudiced, yet he was equally so, and only when he realised this would he be able to overcome it. It was not single-minded and dedicated singers whom he despised, but a neurotic woman who had believed that without her voice she did not exist and who, because of this belief, had refused to accept the fact that her voice was going. Once Paul could be made to see this, he would no longer feel bitter against all women who wanted to pursue a career in conjunction with marriage.

'Don't look so upset,' he whispered. 'I didn't tell you about Helga to make you sad but because I want you to understand me, the way I feel I understand you.'

'You don't know me at all,' she cried.

'I do,' he said, 'and I would like to know you better.'

With a sense of inevitability she found herself being drawn into his hold. Wrapped round by his strong enveloping arms and held close to his heavily thudding heart, she knew she was at last in her rightful place. His lips came down to rest on hers and she opened her mouth to his. Her hands came up inside his jacket and felt the warmth of his skin through the fine silk of his shirt. He moved convulsively at her touch, no longer the controlled man she had always seen but someone inflamed by passion. His hands moved across her back and then came up to the curve of her breasts.

'What are you doing to me?' he said huskily, raising his mouth from hers.

'The same as you're doing to me!'

He gave a soft laugh. 'I seem to have chosen the most inauspicious moment to kiss you. Maggie will be back at any moment.'

'Here I am!' his daughter said as if on cue. 'Sandy did it on the lawn. Isn't he the cleanest dog you've ever known?'

'The cleanest,' Sharon said, drawing back sharply and glancing at Paul.

He gave her a gentle smile and went to the door. 'I'll see you later,' he murmured, and went out.

'What were you and Daddy talking about?' Maggie asked. 'You look all red and funny. Was he in one of his tempers with you?'

'Of course not. Anyway, your father hasn't got a temper.'

'Yes, he has.'

'Well, he wasn't in one with me.' Deliberately Sharon set about clearing up the table. This was her third attempt to do so and she smiled at the thought.

'What's the joke?' Maggie asked.

'No joke,' Sharon said ecstatically. 'I'm just happy.'

CHAPTER TEN

SHARON went down early to dinner that night, but did not have a chance to see Paul. There was a dress rehearsal for *Norma*, Goodwin told her, and Mr. Sanderson had been called over to mediate in a row that had flared up between Tibor, the director, and the set designer. She went into the drawing room to await his return, and was lost in the memory of being held in his arms when the sound of high heels tapping on the parquet floor alerted her to the presence of Honor Macklin.

'Paul not down yet?' the American questioned, the long skirts of her sleek dress settling around her as she sat down.

'He's gone over to the theatre. Would you like me to telephone through and tell him you're here?'

'Gracious, no. I'll be staying tonight, so there's no hurry for me to see him. During the season I tend to drive down when the mood takes me. It's almost my home from home.'

Sharon said nothing, convinced she was being subtly put in her place. Beneath her lashes she glanced at the woman. Not a hair was out of place and her make-up was the work of a craftsman. What did Paul see in her, and what had kept them friends for such a long time? Honor was not a career woman, of course, which must have counted in her favour, and coming from a wealthy family and then marrying into one equally well endowed, she had never worked in her life.

'I must say, you've made a great improvement in Margaret,' the woman said. 'She is almost civil to me these days.'

'She just needed affection.'

'Really? I thought her father gives her more than enough.'

'There's a difference between love and indulgence.'

'You aren't suggesting her father doesn't love her?'

'Of course not, but she needed a different sort of love.'

Bored with the subject of Maggie, Honor Macklin yawned delicately, 'I think I'll wander over to the theatre and see how long Paul will be.'

'I'll come with you,' Sharon surprised herself by saying, and seemed to surprise Honor Macklin too, for her narrow brows rose, though she uttered no word.

It was an unusually warm night for the time of year, with a soft dampness in the air which gave lustre to the grass and the pebbles on the driveway. The sky was peppered with stars and between them flickered the red lights of an aeroplane winking its way towards Heathrow. Skirting the main lawn that bordered the terrace, they passed through the arched wooden door that gave on to the Elizabethan garden. Some of the trees were skilfully illumined and the garden itself could have served as a stage for Benjamin Britten's *Midsummer Night's Dream*.

Oblivious of the beauty around her, Honor walked at a brisk pace, and within a moment the theatre and its adjacent buildings loomed into sight. Only now did one become conscious of other sounds on the insect-droning air, and realise that one was approaching a world inhabited by some sixty volatile people with almost as many different nationalities, making the whole complex a veritable Tower of Babel. Small wonder that Paul was frequently called on to act as referee. The amazing thing was that he had not yet been involved in a murder! Sharon said as much to Honor and the woman gave a cool laugh.

'If I had to cope with all these people, I'd have committed murder long ago. But Paul is the most even-tempered person in the world.'

'Have you known him long?' Sharon asked.

'I met him the year he got married. I divorced my husband the same year that Helga left Pailings. But it's only in the last three years that we have become so—so close.'

'So you knew his wife?' Sharon said deliberately.

'As well as one *could* know her. She had no time for women.'

Like you, Sharon mused, but kept the words to herself. They had reached the theatre and Honor led the way in. It was full of people, though the interest was focused on the stage, where Tibor and a man with long grey-blond hair were arguing furiously. Paul was standing to one side, arms crossed over his chest, the way he usually stood when he was biding his time. If he had come here to mediate, he did not seem to be doing very well, Sharon thought, but even as she watched, he strolled over to the men and lifted his hand.

'You are both right in what you want to do,' he said firmly. 'But since we can't stage *Norma* twice—each time differently—I suggest we do it Tibor's way at tomorrow's dress rehearsal, and Helmut's way at the rehearsal after that.'

'Who will make the decision which one we finally do?' Tibor demanded.

'Both of you. When you have each staged the opera the way you wish to do it, you will then be able to decide which way works the best for this theatre. You are both intelligent men of integrity, and I'm sure that whichever one of you gives in will do so because you are big enough to recognise that someone else's idea is more workable for a Pailings performance.'

'What a fabulous choice of adjectives,' Honor murmured. 'It's far easier to accept that someone else has a more workable idea than to admit they have a better one!'

'Did he learn his diplomacy the hard way?' Sharon asked with some amusement.

'That's like asking which came first—the chicken or the

egg! Paul is Paul.'

Honor moved gracefully down the aisle in his direction, and as she came within a few feet of him he came down the steps at the side of the stage to greet her. Sharon remained hidden behind several people, reluctant to go forward. If only she could have seen Paul on his own! She was a fool to have come here like this. She edged back up the aisle, stopping as she bumped against someone and knowing even before she turned that it was Tony.

'I've just been phoning the house to speak to you,' he exclaimed. 'I was hoping you would come and have supper with me.'

'I can't.'

'Why not?' He pulled her arm through his. 'You don't have to eat supper at the house every night. You argue too much, *cara*, and you have been avoiding me the last few days.'

'I have a job to do.'

'But not day *and* night. Surely you are free once Maggie is in bed? It isn't good for you to stay in the house all the time. You should get out and see people.'

'There are enough people to see here.'

'I was thinking of me,' he reproached.

Since this was exactly what she was trying to avoid, she could not help but look grim, and as he saw it, his small mouth pursed with displeasure.

'What must I do to make you like me?' he demanded. 'In college you were never as cold as you are now. Why are you different?'

'I'm not different.'

'But you were my friend in those days.'

'I'm still your friend. Oh, Tony,' she said in exasperation, 'I wish you'd leave me alone!'

She tried to pull away from him, but the gesture only made him angrier. 'The more you try to escape me, the more I want you.'

'Must you talk to me like someone in a cheap melodrama?'

131

His face went bright red and any humour he had disappeared beneath his punctured ego. He did not love her, of that she was sure, but he could not accept the knowledge that she did not want him. Too late she realised that the best way of dealing with him would be to fawn all over him. Men like Tony did not appreciate an easy conquest, and a few weeks of her devotion would probably have been enough to make him tired of her. In college he had shown the same persistence to girls who did not want him, ignoring the few who had fallen prey to his charms.

'Dear Tony,' she said quickly, 'can't you see that you make me shy? I'm not used to people showing their feelings the way you do.'

With a suddenness that made her want to giggle, his scowl became a glow of pleasure. 'What a fool I am not to have guessed it before! But I never knew you were shy. At college you were always so full of fun, and with so many boy-friends.'

'Safety in numbers,' she said quickly. 'Didn't you guess?'

He squeezed her hand. 'You have no need to be frightened of me. I would never hurt you. I love you, *cara*. You are beautiful and you sing like a dream. In future we must work together. When you have your voice back I will get you a job at La Scala. I know the director and I am going there myself when this season ends.'

He looked past her and his smile changed, telling her that Paul and Honor had come to stand beside them. Conscious of Tony still holding her hand, she quickly pulled it free.

'Don't let *us* interrupt you,' Honor drawled.

'Perhaps you can help me,' Tony said. 'I am trying to persuade Sharon to have dinner with me. I have discovered an excellent Italian restaurant in Haywards Heath. They do a *lasagne* that is superb.' He kissed his hand to his lips and then clicked his fingers. 'Perhaps you will *all* come as my guests? I will ring up and book a table. We can be there in half an hour.'

'Not tonight, I'm afraid,' Paul said. 'I've already made

arrangements.'

'But Sharon is free, I hope? She feels guilty at leaving your daughter, but I——'

'Tony, please,' Sharon interrupted, but had no chance to say more, for Paul cut directly across her to speak to the Italian.

'Sharon has no need to feel guilty. She is perfectly free to go out once Maggie is settled for the night.' Cool grey eyes swivelled to meet Sharon's blue ones. 'You may go out every night if you wish.'

'You see!' Tony said triumphantly to her. 'I told you Mr. Sanderson wouldn't object.'

'But *I* object,' she flared. 'I *don't* want to have dinner with you! It has nothing to do with my leaving Maggie.'

She turned on her heels and stormed out of the theatre, furious with Tony and hurt by Paul who had made her position even more difficult. Hadn't she already told him she didn't want to go out with another man? Hadn't she made it perfectly clear that she regarded Tony as a friend, and a not very good one at that? Tears blurred her vision and momentarily she slowed her pace as she came out of the foyer. Her name was called, but she ignored it, and only when it was called again, more insistently, did she half turn, knowing she had to obey the summons.

'Yes?' she asked as Paul came abreast of her. 'What do you want?'

'Why are you in such a temper?'

'Don't you know?'

'Because of Tony? I'm sorry if I said the wrong thing, but he gave the impression that you wanted to go with him.'

'Tony is adept at giving the wrong impression.' She was still too angry to hide how she felt. 'How can you be so blind? Don't you know I would rather be with you?'

He looked at her in silence and they seemed to be standing in an oasis of their own making, set apart from the people milling around them.

'I love him,' she thought exultantly. 'I love him more

133

than I ever thought it possible to love a man.' It had nothing to do with who he was or what he was. It was a blind, unreasoning emotion that had been there—she now realised —from the moment she had fallen out of the tree and landed at his feet. Call it what one liked: chemical attraction, sexual awareness or mental stimulation; it all led to the same conclusion: she wanted to spend the rest of her life with him. It did not matter whether or not he loved her in return or could offer nothing more than an intermittent friendship. So desperately did she wish to remain with him that she would stay at Pailings for as long as he let her and in whatever capacity he delegated for her. Aware of the depths of her feelings she was too overcome to speak; nor could she have moved had her life depended on it. All she could do was to stand there staring at him, her lips parted, her eyes brilliant.

'I am a fool, aren't I?' he said huskily.

'Yes, you are,' she whispered, and felt his hand grip her elbow tightly as he guided her down the steps.

From the corner of her eye she glimpsed Honor and Tony coming behind her. He was scowling with temper and Sharon knew that in running away from him she had totally negated her earlier flattery. She sighed. Despite her dislike of him she would have to talk to him again and beg him to keep her secret. There was too much at stake for her to let Tony ruin it. She gave him a tentative smile as he approached, but he met it with a black look.

'Why don't you join us for dinner?' Paul asked easily. 'Then I won't feel guilty at refusing your invitation.'

'Do join us,' Honor added. 'Then we'll be able to take you up on your offer of *lasagne* another night instead.'

Instantly Tony was full of smiles and the four of them set off in the direction of the house. Sharon walked beside Paul, but to her surprise Honor and Tony dragged behind, so that within a moment they had fallen out of earshot.

'Inviting our temperamental young tenor to dine with us seemed the best thing to do in the circumstances,' Paul explained softly. 'It will at least ensure that he doesn't sulk

134

for the rest of the week or take out his temper on you.'

'I have no intention of letting him take it out on me—not any more.'

'Meaning that he has done so before?'

She clenched her hands. How quick Paul was at picking up nuances! She glanced at him, loving the seriousness of his profile which she glimpsed in the darkness. Her longing to tell him the truth about herself was so strong that the words trembled on her tongue, held back only by the knowledge that when she did make her confession she wanted to do so when they were alone with no chance of being interrupted. Would he be angry, or would she be able to make him see that her subterfuge had been undertaken only to enable her to live in a world of music at a time when she was bereft of it, and not in order to further her career?

She stole another look at him. He liked her and was attracted to her, of that she had no doubt. But whether the attraction could become more lasting was something she did not know.

'I asked you a question,' he repeated.

She thought quickly and then gave a rueful smile.

'I can't remember what it was.'

He grunted. 'You gave me the impression that you were afraid of Tony. But now I think you've changed, and I'm curious to know if I am right.'

'Yes, you are. I *was* worried by Tony, but now I realise it was childish of me. The best way to control him is not to give him the chance of bullying you.'

'Is that what he was doing?' Paul snapped.

'It was my own fault,' she said quickly, 'but it won't happen again.'

'How well do you know him?'

Here again was her opportunity to tell the truth, but Honor Macklin's silvery laugh, close at hand, kept her silent.

'You did say you knew him in London,' Paul went on.

'Yes, I did. When he was a student there. He studied at the Radley College of Music and——'

135

'You were attracted by an impecunious and handsome young tenor,' Paul concluded.

'Do you find that difficult to understand?'

'Why should I? Acting and singing are glamorous professions. It has an aura that excites the layman. It's only when you look behind the excitement and glamour that you discover the hard work and learn that the stars you worship are ordinary mortals with ordinary tempers.'

'You don't have to tell me *that*,' she said drily. 'I soon saw through the glamour.'

'I'm glad. It would have been a pity if you had gone on being stage-struck. Now you are interested in the things that matter. You care about children, you love the country and I know you love my home.'

'Who wouldn't? Pailings is beautiful.'

'But you see it as a home,' he persisted, 'and not as an opera house in which you could fulfil ambitious dreams.'

The words chilled her, showing her that his thoughts were still with the woman he had married; the woman who had only loved him because he could further her career; a woman whose ego had been too big for her to recognise that her talent had gone.

'You still have a habit of judging all women by your wife,' she said haltingly. 'Don't you think that's unfair?'

'Old pains die hard,' he admitted. 'And don't forget that since Helga left me, plenty of other women have shown their eagerness to fill her place—all of them ambitious singers, all of them loving me because of what they believed I could do for them.'

'Did you give them a chance to love you for yourself?' she burst out. 'You're so eager to prove yourself right. How do you know you haven't misjudged some of the women who—who said they were in love with you?'

'Give me the credit for knowing the difference between genuine love and cupboard love.'

'*Do* you know the difference?'

'I think I do—now.' In the darkness his hand reached out

136

for hers, his fingers twining through her own, strong and warm.

'I must talk to you, Paul,' she whispered.

'You are doing so.'

'I mean alone. I have something to——'

'Paul, honey?' Honor called, and he stopped and looked in her direction, waiting until she and Tony came abreast of them.

'What is it?' he asked.

'I was just telling Tony about the new rehearsal rooms you're planning to build this winter. Aren't you going to put them up here?'

'Beyond the trees,' Paul pointed across the lawn. 'Linked to the present rehearsal room by an underground passage.'

'I don't know where you find the finance,' Tony commented. His good humour was entirely restored, and as the clouds scudded away from the face of the moon, Sharon saw that he was smiling.

'Paul has lots of friends in the City,' Honor explained.

'It's clever of you to combine your two careers,' Tony said. 'Opera entrepreneur and financier.'

'If I weren't the latter, I might not be the former.' Paul continued to walk again and Sharon had the impression that he found it an effort to be polite to Tony. The knowledge delighted her, confirming her in her belief that he was jealous of Tony. But she must show him that he had no need to be jealous of any man. *He* was the only one who mattered in her life; now and forever. The house came in sight, the lighted windows welcoming them.

'You are seeing Pailings at its best,' Paul murmured to her, his voice so muted that she alone could hear it. 'You might not find it so lovely in the winter.'

'I think I would love it more when there are no strangers to disturb its tranquillity.'

'I hope so.' He touched her arm lightly, then dropped his hand to his side and walked silently across the lawn to the terrace.

137

CHAPTER ELEVEN

SHARON'S longing to tell Paul the truth about herself was thwarted by circumstance. She had hoped to do so after dinner, when Tony returned to the opera annexe and Honor retired to her room. But hardly was dinner over when Paul received an urgent call from Munich which necessitated him flying to Germany first thing in the morning. It meant his driving immediately to London Airport, where he would spend the night at a nearby hotel and catch the first available flight out.

'It's better than getting up at the crack of dawn and driving through the mist,' he explained.

'Can't someone else go to Munich for you?' Honor asked. 'You keep a kennel full of dogs, yet you do the barking yourself.'

He grinned at the comment. 'As I'm the leader of the pack, I like to bark the loudest!' He glanced from Tony to Sharon. 'I hope you will forgive me if I say goodnight now? I have several documents to take with me and I must sort them out.'

Sharon watched him leave the room with a sense of apprehension, and a little later she made an excuse to leave too, pretending she wanted to see if Maggie was safely asleep, but going instead to the library in search of Paul.

He was busy at his desk, so preoccupied that she suddenly felt nervous for daring to interrupt him. Though she herself had acknowledged her love for him, he had given no similar indication, beyond showing that he liked her and found her desirable, and to openly declare what she felt for him suddenly seemed foolish and lacking in pride.

He looked up and saw her standing uncertainly by the door. 'Yes?' he said impatiently. 'What is it?'

Numbly she went on staring at him. She could not tell him anything that was in her mind; neither her love nor the confession that she was a singer. Now was not the time, when his thoughts were already preoccupied with the problems he would be facing in Munich.

'It's nothing,' she said awkwardly. 'I—I just wondered if there was anything I could do to help?'

'No, thanks.' He stuffed some papers in a briefcase.

'How long will you be away?'

'A couple of days.' He half turned, an odd expression on his face. 'Don't look so miserable. I'm not going to the ends of the earth.'

She forced a smile to her lips. 'It will be lonely here without you.'

'With the cast and orchestra here?' he snapped his brief-case shut and glanced at his watch.

'It's only nine o'clock,' she burst out. 'Why are you in such a hurry?'

'I'm meeting Carl Frankel at the airport hotel in an hour. I have several things to discuss with him before flying to Munich.'

'Is it some sort of crisis?'

'A spot of bother over Emily Schmitt's contract with me,' he explained, naming a world-famous coloratura. 'As I've already waited three years to have her sing here, I don't intend to be done out of her services by her sharp little agent!'

'Will seeing her make any difference?'

'I hope so. I intend to make it quite clear that if she breaks her contract with me, she'll find it very difficult to get work in any other opera house of repute.'

'Could you carry out such a threat?'

'No,' he admitted.

'Then is it wise to bluff?'

'It's worth the chance. Singers are temperamental and nervous people, Sharon, and even the possibility that I can cause trouble for her may be enough to make her decide not to break her contract with me.'

'You sound as if you enjoy fighting.'

'I don't like being made a fool of, and too many singers think that the end justifies the means.'

'Sometimes it does,' she said, thinking of herself.

'Never. If you do something knowing it to be wrong, you have no right to expect any clemency if you're found out.'

'What a harsh thing to say!'

'I don't see why. Emily made a contract with me and I'm going to see she sticks to it. Just because she has received a better offer from someone else, it doesn't give her the right to let me down.' He came across to the door and Sharon stepped back to let him pass. 'Don't look so distressed by it,' he said with a slight smile. 'You're too soft-hearted. Emily Schmitt is a tough woman, despite her angelic voice, and a bit of plain speaking won't do her any harm.'

Sharon kept silent, knowing it was foolish to argue with him. Besides, they were arguing at cross purposes. He was only concerned with the singer and her contract, whereas she herself was thinking of her own position and the lies she had told in order to obtain it. The end did justify the means. Paul had to be made to see that. If only she could tell him the truth now!

'Goodbye, Sharon,' he said. 'Take care of Maggie while I'm away.'

'You know I will.'

He touched her cheek lightly with his finger, but had no chance to speak, for the drawing room door opened and Honor came out. If she was surprised to see Sharon beside Paul, she did not say so, though the flash of temper in her eyes made comment unnecessary.

'Is the chauffeur taking you to the airport?' she enquired, 'or would you like me to drive you?'

'I'm driving myself. I'll leave the car at the hotel.'

He strode to the front door and only as he opened it did he glance again in Sharon's direction. But he did not speak, merely raised his arm in farewell before going down the steps.

To hide the swift dejection that welled up in her, she turned and ran upstairs. She had said she was going to see if Maggie was sleeping and it would be as well to do as she had said. The little girl was almost hidden in a mound of blankets, and Sharon eased them away and gently touched the fine hair splayed out on the pillow. Even in the short time she had been with her, the child was less tense and wilful. She responded to affection like a puppy but, like a puppy, she still required a great deal of affection and careful handling. It was wrong to send her to boarding school. She needed the atmosphere of a home and the constant attention of loving parents. Even one loving parent. Sharon determined to make Paul realise this. He loved his daughter and he would want to do what was best for her.

The knowledge that Paul was speeding away from her in the darkness of the night suddenly filled her with fear. If only she could have told him all that was in her heart before he had gone away! She needed to know what he thought of her and if there was a chance that her own love for him could ever be reciprocated. To believe that he loved her already was unwise, for it was based only on her need to think so and not on reality. Yet he had held her in his arms and kissed her; had shown he found her desirable. Surely he would not have done that unless she meant something to him? Yet men were frequently governed by their emotions and could say and do things that they did not mean once their emotion was under control. Somehow she could not believe this applied to Paul, more particularly as she was working for him. Her very position in his home would make him careful not to give her the wrong idea. He did feel something deep about her. She was convinced of it.

Smiling ruefully at the way her thoughts fluctuated, she went downstairs and found Honor and Tony in the drawing room deep in conversation. It died the moment she came in, but resumed again almost at once, though Sharon felt the resumption was forced and that they had been talking about something quite different before she had come in. Tony looked vaguely uneasy and refused to meet her eye, and she wondered if he regretted his outburst of temper earlier that evening.

She had no chance to ask him, for when he stood up to leave it was Honor who went with him to the door, return-

141

ing with the look of a cat who had discovered a bowl of cream.

'Such a nice young man,' she purred. 'I believe you know him rather well?'

'I'm afraid that's wishful thinking on Tony's part.'

'You could do worse, you know.'

Sharon bit her lip, not sure whether to tell Honor the truth about herself. It seemed a logical time to do so, yet she was reluctant to speak without first telling Paul.

'I'm going to bed,' Honor yawned. 'Country air always makes me tired.'

'I'll come up too,' Sharon said, and turned off the lights.

At the top of the stairs Honor paused. 'I won't be staying here now that Paul has gone. I'll drive back to London in the morning.'

Sharon was delighted, but kept it from showing on her face. 'Then I'll say goodbye now, Mrs. Macklin, in case I don't see you before you go.'

'I'll be back at the end of the week—when Paul returns.'

There was a slight difference in the timbre of the lilting voice, but Sharon could not define what it signified, and she forgot about it as she went down the corridor to her room.

Her sleep that night was punctuated by uneasy dreams, with Paul's presence felt but never seen and Tony her constant companion. Honor was in her dreams too, but she never spoke, and merely seemed to hover on the edge of each scene, always dressed in black and always looking amused.

It was still early when Sharon awoke. It was too early for Honor to have left the house and, unwilling to see the woman again, she remained in her bedroom until her clock showed nine. Only then did she go in search of Maggie, and found she had already eaten breakfast and was walking the puppy along the drive and training him on the lead. Sharon went out on the steps and Maggie saw her and came running over.

'Daddy has gone away,' she cried. 'He left me a letter. I found it on my bedside table when I woke up this morning.'

Sharon was glad Paul had found the time to make such a gesture, and her love for him was so strong that it made her tremble. 'I know, dear. He told me he hopes to be home at the end of the week.'

'I don't mind him going away now I have you to look after me.'

'That's a nice thing to say.'

'You won't leave me, will you, Sharon?'

'You will be leaving me at the end of the summer. I'm sure you're looking forward to it. You will make so many friends at your new school that——'

'I don't want to go away to school! I want to stay here with you. I've already told Daddy and he promised to think about it.'

Sharon's heart gave a leap, but she kept her voice steady. 'It might be difficult for him to change his mind. He has already made the arrangements.'

'He can unmake them. He said he would see if I could be a weekly boarder instead.' Maggie nestled against Sharon's side in an unusual gesture of affection. 'Daddy said I wanted the best of both worlds. I was going to ask him what that meant, but I forgot, and when I remembered again, he wasn't there. Do you know what he meant, Sharon?'

'I think so,' Sharon smiled, 'but I'll leave your daddy to explain it to you.'

Maggie tilted back her head and looked up. Her eyes, so like her father's, made Sharon long to hug her, and she did so briefly.

'Go and play with Sandy before he eats his way through the lead,' she suggested, and watched to make sure Maggie was absorbed again with the puppy before returning to the house for her own breakfast.

It was odd that Paul had made no mention to her of Maggie's request, but the answer he had given to his daughter filled her with pleasure and made the world suddenly seem a happier place. It prompted her to go in search of Tony. Now that she had made up her mind to tell Paul that she was a singer, the Italian was no longer a threat to

143

her and could not command her attention any more. Once he accepted this it might be possible for them to remain friends, but she had no intention of being at his beck and call or allowing him to flirt with her. What a fool she had been to give him the opportunity of putting her in such a position! The moment she had seen him in the drawing room at Pailings she should have known he was the sort of man who would take a mile if given an inch. She should have made it clear at their first meeting that she would rather tell Paul the truth about herself than bind Tony's silence with false friendship. Still, better late than never.

But Sharon's intention of clearing the air with Tony was delayed by learning that he had left for London.

'He isn't wanted for rehearsals for the rest of the week,' the accompanist, Gladys Pugh, informed her. 'So he went away for a couple of days.'

Sharon wondered whether his decision had anything to do with her quarrel with him. Perhaps recognising her change of mood, he had recognised too that she would not be amenable to his company and could well have decided to go in search of someone else. Knowing Tony, he would not be short of girl-friends in London. What a relief it would be if this were true.

'He left with Mrs. Macklin,' the woman continued. 'I saw them drive off in her car.'

This was a development Sharon had not expected. Surely Tony had not turned his attention to the American? Of course there was no reason why he should not do so, for she was beautiful and intelligent—too intelligent, one would have thought, to be interested in Tony.

'Do you want to leave a message in case Tony rings here?' Gladys Pugh asked.

'No. What I have to say to him can wait till he comes back.'

'I hear Mr. Sanderson has gone away too. He's having some trouble with Emily Schmitt, isn't he?'

'I'm not sure,' Sharon hedged, reluctant to gossip.

'She's a fool if she tries to cross swords with him,' the

144

pianist went on. 'She'll really get cut up if she does.'

'Mr. Sanderson isn't as ruthless as all that,' Sharon protested.

'He is where the company is concerned. And I should think he's the same about everything that concerns him. He's a tough man, Sharon. Don't be misled by his charming manner. Underneath he's ruthless and determined.'

'If he weren't he would never have got the opera company going,' Sharon said evenly.

'Maybe, but remember that determined men are seldom kind.'

'Are you warning me about him?' Sharon asked, trying to keep her voice light.

'I have a feeling the warning has come too late. I watched you with him in the theatre last night. There were sparks between you.'

'If I was sparking, it was because I was furious with Tony.'

'Your anger with Tony had nothing to do with it,' the pianist said positively. 'It was a different kind of sparkle.'

'Why shouldn't I like Mr. Sanderson?'

'I don't want you to be hurt. He's years older than you, Sharon.'

'Only twelve,' she said quickly.

'But a lifetime more sophisticated. Don't forget I saw how he coped when his wife left him.'

'That should make you have *more* compassion for him—not less! You should want him to be happy again.'

'He *is* happy,' the woman said in surprise. 'He has stacks of money, a wonderful home, work he enjoys and a hobby he adores. What else does he need?'

'A woman he can love.'

'What about Mrs. Macklin?'

'If Mr. Sanderson loved her, he would have already....' Sharon stopped, afraid that to say more would give away her own feelings. 'I don't know why we're gossiping like a couple of old women!'

'Because I'm trying to stop you from falling for your

145

boss,' Gladys Pugh said bluntly.

But for Sharon the warning had come too late. She loved
Paul and would always compare him with every other man
she met. It was a chastening thought, and she tried to find
some comfort in the conversation she had had with him on
the way back from the rehearsal to the house the night of
his departure. She was certain he had wanted to say more to
her than he had, and wondered if his silence stemmed from
the belief that it was disloyal to tell a woman one loved her
while one's former love was still a guest in your home.
Knowing Paul, she could well imagine him thinking this
way. But when he returned from Munich, Honor would not
be here, and there would then be no reason for him to remain silent.

Looking at her reflection in a downstairs mirror as she
returned to Pailings, she was faintly reassured. She did not
have Honor's elegance nor the beauty of the many women
with whom Paul mixed in his business life, but she had an
indefinable quality that came from personality as well as
good looks, a quality that would last when mere beauty had
faded. She ran her fingers through her chestnut gold hair
and the feel of it, thick and silky, gave her more confidence.
She only hoped she could remain confident until Paul returned.

'I love him,' she said to herself, 'and I know he isn't
indifferent to me.'

But was it love on his part, or infatuation? Was it something he was ready to enjoy only while she was staying here
with Maggie, or would it lead to her remaining here to
share his life? These were questions only Paul could
answer, and she found herself counting the hours until she
saw him again.

CHAPTER TWELVE

Sharon and Maggie were in the library listening to some records when Paul telephoned to speak to his daughter.

They chatted for several minutes, and Maggie regaled him with the happenings of her day: Sandy was learning new tricks; she had cut out another dress for herself and was going to sew it tomorrow.

'Now I'm listening to music in the library with Sharon,' she concluded, 'and then I'm going to bed.' Her pointed little face tilted enquiringly as she listened to her father speak, then she giggled and held out the receiver to Sharon. 'Daddy wants to speak to you.'

Nervously Sharon took the telephone, her voice shaky as she said hello.

'Do you know this is the first time I've heard your voice without being able to see your face?' Paul said. 'It sounds quite different.'

'In what way?'

'Like a little girl's. But then you are a little girl, aren't you; twelve years younger than I am.'

'I don't feel it,' she said quickly.

'Is that because you feel older than your age or I appear younger?'

'A little of both. I think we meet in the middle.'

He chuckled, and the sound warmed her and made her lose her nervousness. 'Have you missed me?' he asked.

'Of course.'

'Aren't you going to ask if I've missed you?'

'I wouldn't have the nerve.'

'I've never known you to be bashful.'

'I'm not,' she protested, 'it's shyness.'

'When I come home, I'll have to see what I can do to overcome that.'

'When *will* you be back?'

'A couple of days. Will you be glad to see me?'

'We both will,' she said composedly.

'But will *you*?'

She let out a sharp sigh. 'Yes. Very much indeed.'

'Oh, Sharon.' His voice was suddenly shaky, and even though they were miles apart, she had a vivid mental picture of him, his grey-flecked head bent towards the telephone, his eyes alight with the quizzical look that she knew so well. 'It's hell talking to you this way,' he said abruptly, 'I'll be back the moment I can, Sharon.'

The receiver clicked and she slowly replaced it. Aware of Maggie watching her, she forced her attention to the child, and was glad when the record on the turntable came to an end and she could busy herself with finding another one. More than ever she was certain Paul loved her. He was not the sort of man to have spoken to her in the way he had just done if she did not mean more to him than his daughter's companion. She hugged the memory of the call to herself, anxious to be alone in her bedroom so that she could examine it afresh, could ponder over each word and nuance like a rabbinical scholar studying the Talmud.

The following day was Saturday and she was so sure Paul would be home in the afternoon that she went up to change before lunch, choosing one of her prettiest dresses: a full-skirted lime green silk one that went well with her tanned skin and clear eyes. Living in the country suited her, and happiness suited her even more, for never had she looked more glowing and vital.

Even Maggie commented on it and kept staring at her in a puzzled way, sensing the excitement yet not knowing what caused it. In the morning they had gone together to watch the final rehearsal of *Norma*, with which the Pailings season would commence on Monday.

'Things will be hectic from now on,' Maggie had informed her in a grown-up voice as they had returned to the house for lunch. 'If the weather is good, some of the audience arrive at lunchtime and spend the whole afternoon here, even though the opera doesn't begin until five-thirty. Lots of them try and get into our house to look around, but

148

Daddy never lets them. Sometimes he gets awfully cross about it.'

'I thought visitors *were* able to go into the house,' Sharon had commented.

'Only at weekends, and then only the music room. They can wander round the gardens and have picnics on the lawn, but no one is ever allowed into Pailings during the week.'

'You'll have to keep Sandy out of the way,' Sharon had warned. 'Otherwise he might make a nuisance of himself.'

'Sandy could never be a nuisance,' Maggie had protested, and had raced ahead with the puppy barking joyfully at her heels.

Sharon thought of this conversation as, luncheon over, she sat on the terrace and watched the sun warming the velvet-smooth grass. How beautifully kept everything was, the lawns as trim as though they had been manicured, the flowerbeds a patchwork quilt of colour and the trees ranged like proud, tall sentinels along the drive. She felt such a deep sense of belonging here that it was difficult to believe she had been here so short a time. Yet if she had not lost her voice she might never have come here at all or—if she had—would have come as a singer and be staying in the annexe, only seeing Pailings itself for the weekly cocktail party which Paul gave for all the cast.

Instead, she was living in his home as a member of his family, with the chance to see him every day and participate in his private life and not merely be part of his hobby. It must be a strain for him to run an opera company as well as a property one, and she wondered whether he worked so hard in an effort to forget his unhappy marriage. She thought of the dead Helga and knew a stab of jealousy. He must have loved the woman very much if he was still so bitter that he had vowed never to love a singer again. Guilt rose high and pushed away her jealousy, and suddenly she was overwhelmingly scared by the way she herself had deceived him. No longer was it a gay and lighthearted deception but—seeing it from his point of view—a deliberate attempt to ingratiate herself with him by use of a lie. Fear

149

brought her to her feet, and the chair went screeching across the stone floor of the terrace. The sound of it drowned the sound of a car engine, and it was only as its gleaming bonnet shone brightly in the sunshine as it curved round the drive that she knew Paul had arrived home.

'Daddy's here!' she called to Maggie, who was sprawled on the grass reading a book, and the child bounded to her feet and raced to meet the car.

Gripped by shyness, Sharon remained where she was, and saw Paul step on to the driveway and stretch himself as though he was tired, before bending to hug his daughter. Then his head turned and she knew he was looking in her own direction. Still she did not move from the terrace, and waited, trembling as if with fever; he patted Maggie's shoulder and then walked slowly across the lawn in her direction. As he came nearer, she saw that his eyes were dark-rimmed with fatigue and that there were tired lines on either side of his mouth.

'I had a feeling you would be back today.' Was this her voice, so breathless and shaky? She cleared her throat. 'Have you had lunch?'

'On the plane. But I could do with some coffee.' He put out a restraining hand as she turned towards the French windows. 'Maggie will get it.' He gave his daughter a push and she ran inside happily.

Aware of Paul still watching her, Sharon sat down and stared everywhere except in his direction.

'Darling, look at me,' he said huskily. 'I've been aching for a sight of those beautiful blue eyes of yours ever since I left you the other night.'

It was the first time he had called her darling and her bones seemed to be made of jelly, dissolving in the heat of her emotions.

'Look at me,' he repeated, and she raised her head and did so, seeing cool grey eyes that were not cool any more, but glowing as though with an inner fire. He leaned towards her, but as he did so Maggie skipped out on to the terrace again.

150

'Coffee will be here in a minute,' she piped. 'Why didn't you tell us you were coming back today, then we could have met you at the airport?'

'I wasn't definitely sure until late last night, and then it was touch and go whether I could get a seat on the plane. As it was, I had to change flights en route.'

'Why did you do that?'

'Because I was in a hurry to get back.'

'To see me?' Maggie asked, twining her arms round his legs.

'To see you,' he replied, but looked over his daughter's head to Sharon, his eyes telling her that the words were meant for her alone. Her cheeks grew pink and he showed awareness of their change of colour by smiling. But Maggie demanded his attention again, begging him to come on the lawn and see the tricks she had taught Sandy in his absence.

'Your father is tired,' Sharon protested. 'Let him have his coffee and a rest. You have plenty of time later on to show him Sandy's tricks.'

'I want to show him now.' Excited at having her father back, Maggie momentarily reverted to the spoiled child. 'You will come on the lawn with me, won't you, Daddy?'

'No, poppet. I'm going to do as Sharon says and have a rest.'

'You're mean!' Maggie cried. 'You're mean and I don't like you.'

'You're mean, but I still like *you*,' her father said calmly. 'Though it won't prevent me from giving you a smack if you don't behave yourself.'

Maggie gaped at him. 'You've *never* smacked me!'

'There's always a first time.'

Maggie's lower lip trembled and she was not a grown-up eight-year-old but a very childish one.

'Your father is only teasing you,' Sharon said quickly, 'and I'm sure you were only teasing him. Fetch Sandy's ball and lead. When your father has had a rest I'm sure he'll want to see Sandy's tricks.'

Happy again, the little girl rushed off, and Paul leaned

151

back in his chair and sighed. 'You're much more patient with Maggie than I am. I wish you'd come here a long time ago—and not just for Maggie's sake,' he added.

Sharon's reply was forestalled by Goodwin's appearance with the coffee tray. He set it on a table and, conscious of Paul watching her, Sharon managed to pour the coffee without spilling any.

'I'm ready when you are, Daddy,' Maggie called from the lawn, and waved the lead which set Sandy barking.

'You have to admit there's a lot to be said for sending her to boarding school,' Paul murmured as he nodded in his daughter's direction to indicate he would soon be joining her.

'She's just excited because you've been away. She's normally very undemanding.'

'Only since you've been here. You've made a world of difference to her.' His voice lowered. 'And a world of difference to *me*.'

Nervously Sharon looked down at the floor.

'I love you,' he whispered, and then set his cup down sharply on the saucer. 'Lord, what a way to tell you! I'd planned to do it tonight, when I had you to myself.'

'Daddy!' Maggie called again. 'We're waiting for you.'

'You see what I mean?' he said despairingly.

'We have plenty of time,' Sharon replied, and lifted her head, her eyes glowing with happiness. 'Oh, Paul, I love you too.'

He caught her hand in a grip that made her wince. 'I'll send Maggie and the dog packing as soon as I can,' he promised. 'I'm darned if I'll wait until she's in bed before I take you in my arms and kiss you.'

As though afraid he might do so now, if he went on standing beside her, he turned and went down the steps. Sharon watched him, unable to believe the happiness that seemed to be hers. Only when she had made her confession would she know complete peace of mind, and she nervously wondered how to tell him. Should she begin by saying she had throat trouble and then lead up to the fact she had been a singer? Or should she say first of all that she could sing and then take the story from there? To and fro her thoughts raced, becoming more complicated with every moment, until she was soon a bundle of nerves and jumped like a startled rabbit as the sharp honk of a klaxon sounded above Sandy's yelps, and she looked up to see a car coming to a stop beside Paul's. The door opened and Honor stepped out, followed by Tony. The two of them walked across the lawn to Paul and Maggie.

'Darling,' Honor said gaily, 'we timed our arrival beautifully.'

'Psychic powers or luck?' he asked as Honor leant forward to have him kiss her cheek.

'A telephone call to Munich,' she replied. 'I expected you to phone to let me know when you were leaving.'

'I never knew I merited such attention.' Paul moved back to the terrace and Honor walked beside him, with Tony a step or two behind.

'Hello, Sharon,' Honor greeted her. 'I'm glad you're here. I have a surprise for you.'

Without knowing why, Sharon felt afraid. She glanced at Tony, but he avoided her eyes, and she saw he was pale and nervous.

'Where is it, Tony?' Honor continued.

He withdrew his hand from his pocket and held out a tape. Honor took it from him and passed it over to Paul.

'For you, darling,' she said. 'My new discovery—a singer you might be able to use for next season.'

Paul looked surprised. 'Since when have you been a talent scout?'

'I'm not. It happened by pure chance and because of Tony. The singer is his discovery.'

Paul turned to the tenor. 'Is he an Italian?'

'It is a she.' Tony's voice was thick and he cleared his throat.

At once Sharon knew the truth. Horror gripped her and she longed to reach out and snatch the tape from Paul's hand. But if she did she would give herself away. All she

153

could do was to remain quiet and watch and wait. And listen, she thought desperately.

Paul walked along the terrace and into the library. Honor followed him, her arm linked through Tony's.

'Do come with us, Sharon,' she called over her shoulder.

Sharon longed to refuse but knew it was impossible. Her teeth bit her lip so hard that she drew blood, but in silence she followed them. No wonder Tony had refused to meet her eyes a moment ago; if conscience had any part in his behaviour he would never be able to meet her eyes again.

Paul switched on the recorder and put on the tape Honor had given him. 'Who am I going to hear?' he asked.

'We'll tell you her name afterwards,' Honor drawled, and sank gracefully into a chair.

Paul pressed the switch and the sound of piano music was heard, followed almost at once by the rich and rounded tones of a beautiful soprano voice. It sang the Countess's aria from *The Marriage of Figaro*, where she sadly mused on her adoration of a husband who no longer loved her.

> *Where are those happy moments,*
> *Of sweetness and pleasure?*
> *Where have they gone,*
> *Those vows of a deceiving tongue?*

The first line told Sharon all she needed to know, and she hid her trembling hands in the folds of her skirt. It was her voice singing the part of the Countess to Tony's Count, at the end of term in their final year at the music college. It was that performance which had brought her to the attention of the man who was now her agent and who, hearing her sing, had prophesied the birth of a new star in the opera firmament. She vaguely remembered that one of the teachers had made a recording of the opera, but she had not bothered to get a copy of it for herself. Now she was hearing it played back for the first time and would have given anything in the world never to have heard it at all, and certainly not in this way.

She raised her head and met Honor's hard brown eyes.

Quickly she looked away, scorning Tony in order to focus on Paul. He was leaning forward, hands clasped loosely together, his whole expression intent.

'You don't need to listen to any more,' Honor's voice cut across the sound and she flipped off the recorder switch.

'Put it on again,' Paul said quietly. 'I'd like to hear it all.'

'Another time, darling. What did you think of it? Have I discovered a star, do you think, or just another voice for the chorus?'

'She is undoubtedly going to be a star,' Paul said. 'The voice has a marvellous tone and quality. I think that—'

'*Madre mia!*' Tony interrupted, and jumped to his feet. 'I cannot do it. I should never have agreed.' He swung round on Honor. 'I was crazy to let you persuade me!'

'It had to come out sooner or later,' Honor retorted, 'and there'll be far less harm done if it comes out now.'

'Would you mind telling me what you're talking about?' Paul asked Tony. 'I take it you have second thoughts about letting me hear this recording. Does that mean the singer isn't free?'

'She is free,' Tony muttered, 'but she isn't singing any more.'

'Only temporarily mute,' Honor intervened. 'She's had some trouble with her throat and isn't allowed to sing for six months. But her voice will be as good as new when she starts again.'

'Then I must arrange to hear her later.' Paul looked at Tony again. 'I take it you know where she is?'

'I—I——'

'In front of you,' Honor interposed.

Paul frowned and glanced from Honor to Tony to Sharon. His eyes widened and then narrowed as he saw the scarlet patches in Sharon's cheeks.

'You?' he said, and the quietness of his voice held the quietness of death. 'Is it you?'

She nodded, unable to speak even had her life depended on it.

155

'Don't you think it was clever of Sharon to come here the way she did?' Honor asked brightly. 'Even though she wasn't allowed to sing for six months she could at least learn a great deal by watching the rehearsals and getting to know everyone. You have to admit it was enterprising.'

'It certainly was.' Paul stood up and lifted the tape from the machine. 'You have an excellent voice, Sharon.'

He looked her fully in the face and she stared back at him. But she felt she was looking at a stranger, for his eyes were like polished steel and no less hard. No need to ask if he were hurt by the disclosure of her identity.

'I was—I was going to tell you.' She stumbled over the words, aware of Tony's heavy breathing behind her and of Honor's look of amusement.

'I'm sure you were,' Paul said politely. 'But now there's no need.' He looked at the tape. 'Do I give this to you or Tony?'

She recoiled from it as if it were a snake, and Tony came forward to take it, glancing at Sharon as he did so.

'You must be feeling very pleased with yourself,' she said huskily.

'You couldn't keep it a secret for ever,' he muttered. 'It was ridiculous of you to go on pretending.' As he spoke he seemed to recover his bravura, becoming the bragging, self-confident Figaro that he was shortly to play. 'Sharon was one of the best students of her year,' he said to Paul. 'When I saw her looking after your daughter I thought it was a joke.'

'The joke seems to have been on me,' Paul replied.

'I didn't intend it as a joke on anyone,' Sharon said desperately. 'I was ordered not to sing for six months and I had to earn a living in the meantime. When this job came up it seemed like fate. You can't blame me for taking it?'

'I'm not blaming you,' Paul said smoothly. 'Anyone in your position would have jumped at the chance of coming here, even though you did have to pretend you weren't a singer.'

'I hadn't intended to keep it a secret. I thought that once

156

I had the job and—and—you learned to—to—trust me, I could tell you the truth. I was going to tell you before you went abroad,' she said swiftly, 'but I didn't get the chance. You've got to believe me, Paul.'

'There's no need to sound so worried,' he was still cool, still looking faintly amused. 'The joke was on me—I'll admit that freely—but it will make an amusing after-dinner story.' He went to the door. 'I must go across to the theatre. I want to look at the bookings.'

'I'll come with you,' Honor said.

'Good.' Paul's mouth curved in what should have been a smile and yet could not have been called so, for it did not change his expression.

Together they went from the room and mutely Tony walked over to the tape recorder and looked at it. 'I meant it as a joke,' he muttered.

'You meant it as a piece of spite,' Sharon said angrily.

'To begin with, yes,' he conceded. 'I was angry with you and I blurted out who you were to Honor. It was the night you refused to have dinner with me.'

'So that was what the two of you were talking about! I had the feeling you were going to make trouble for me, but I never thought you capable of being quite so rotten!'

'What's rotten about it? In a few months you'll be singing again and Paul is the obvious man to hear you. If he likes your voice and asks you to come here, you'll be made.'

'Can you honestly see him asking me now? Didn't you see the way he looked at me? He hates me for the trick I played on him!'

'His pride is hurt, nothing more. He'll get over it in a day.'

'How little you know him,' she said bitterly, and burst into tears. It was a long time since she had cried with such abandon. Even the misery of learning that she could not sing for six months had been nothing compared with the anguish that filled her now.

Tony stared at her in astonishment. Then as her crying continued, the astonishment turned to contrition and he knelt at her side. 'I'm sure he'll forgive you, Sharon. After all, you've done no harm.'

'You don't understand . . . he thought I was different . . . that I liked him for himself—not because of the opera company.'

'He won't let that affect his judgement. He's always searching for good singers. He won't let you go because you played a trick on him.'

'He will, he will.' She rocked backwards and forwards, too distraught to care what she said. Pretence seemed a weak and feeble thing; unworthy of the love she felt for Paul. 'I love him!' she cried. 'I love him, and now you've made him hate me.'

'It wasn't my idea you kept quiet about your voice.'

'I had to keep quiet,' she wailed. 'It was the only way of staying here. I was going to tell him the truth tonight. If only you and Honor had come tomorrow instead of today!' Her tears fell faster and she buried her head in her hands.

Tony touched her hair with a fumbling gesture. 'I had no idea you were serious about him. I thought it was a game you were playing.'

With an effort she stemmed her tears, but her throat was thick with them. 'I love him. I didn't intend to, it just happened.'

'Does he love you?'

At her nod, he caught her hands. 'Then you've nothing to worry about. A few more tears from you, a little more explanation and all will be forgiven. After all, what you did wasn't a crime.' He got to his feet, so concerned for her that he did not bother to dust the knees of his trousers. 'If I had known you were serious about him, I wouldn't have done it,' he admitted. 'Mrs. Macklin must have guessed, though, and used *me* to hurt you.' He kicked mutely at the fender. 'She is a bitch, that one.'

'She wants Paul and she'll stop at nothing to get him.'

'She hasn't got him so far. Come with me to the theatre, Sharon. You may have a chance to talk to Mr. Sanderson there.'

'I don't want to see him in front of anyone else. I must talk to him alone.'

For a few seconds he looked at her, his swarthy face full of contrition, then he half raised his arm in farewell and left her alone.

Sharon went to her room to wash her face. Her skin was blotched from crying and her eyes were red, but somehow her appearance did not seem to matter, and afraid to stay upstairs in case Paul returned and she did not have a chance to see him, she hurried down again. Maggie was crossing the hall, holding Sandy.

'He fell in the lake,' she explained, 'and I'm taking him upstairs to have a bath. Will you hold him for me, Sharon?'

'I can't, I have a headache. Ask one of the maids.'

It was so rare for Sharon to refuse to be with Maggie that the little girl looked at her in surprise. 'Would you like me to stay with you and keep you company?'

'No, dear. I would rather be by myself.' Sandy began to wag his tail and drops of muddy water fell on the floor. 'For heaven's sake, take him upstairs before he makes a mess everywhere.'

'Will you come up afterwards?'

'Yes,' Sharon said, and forced herself to watch until Maggie had rushed upstairs and disappeared from sight. Then she went into the library again and stood by the window, watching anxiously for Paul's return. She did not know how long she stood there, but her back was aching by the time she saw his tall, upright figure walking along the drive. He had discarded his jacket somewhere and had undone his tie against the heat. The top button of his shirt was undone too and she saw the strong column of his throat. Was the hair of his chest flecked with grey too? she wondered, and again felt the sting of tears in her eyes. Hastily she blinked them away and ran into the hall as he came in.

'I thought you would be waiting for me,' he said quietly. 'I must talk to you.'

'We have nothing to say to each other.'

'I want to explain why I——'

'Explanations aren't necessary or needed. I know exactly why you came here. I know exactly why you pretended to be in love with me.'

'I wasn't pretending,' she choked. 'It's true. I do love you.' She held out her hands to him. 'You have to believe me, Paul, I do love you.'

He drew in a sharp breath. It tightened his mouth and made him look grim. 'Maybe you do love me in your way. As Paul Sanderson, head of the Pailings Opera Company, I'm a very lovable man.'

'That isn't what I meant!' she cried.

'Do you expect me to believe *anything* you say?' he said savagely. 'For heaven's sake, Sharon, I wasn't born yesterday! I'm a power in the world of opera. I can't break a singer, but I can certainly make one. You know that as well as I do.'

'That wasn't why I came here.'

'Then why did you keep your profession a secret?'

'Because you wouldn't have let me work for you. Mrs. Macklin said——'

'Forget what Honor said. I can see why you kept quiet in the beginning, but I can't understand why you didn't tell me the truth weeks ago.'

'I was afraid.'

'Afraid that I wasn't sufficiently under your spell? Is that why you kept quiet? Did you want me to fall in love with you before you told me the truth?' He strode over and caught her in a vicious grip. 'Don't bother answering me, I can see it in your eyes. From the minute we met, you knew I was attracted to you and you played on it. But you wanted to be a hundred per cent sure of me. That was why you waited.'

'You speak as if I planned it all,' she cried. 'But I didn't. I didn't know you were attracted to me and I didn't know I was going to fall in love with you. But when I did, I was so afraid that I . . . that I . . . I was going to tell you the truth the night you found me quarrelling with Tony. But then you went to Munich and I didn't have the chance.'

'You would never have found the chance,' he burst out, and shook her hard. 'You'd have waited until it was too late for me to do anything about it—until I was married to you!'

'Married!' she cried. 'Oh, Paul, I——'

'Don't look at me like that,' he grated. 'It's over. Finished. The girl I thought you were doesn't even exist.'

'Of course I exist,' she cried. 'My being a singer hasn't changed anything.'

'It has changed everything.' He dropped his hands away from her and walked into the library. She followed him, but he did not turn round, and instead stared at the empty grate as though seeing his future in it. 'After Helga left me, I vowed I would never fall in love with a singer again. That I would never trust any woman who had a career or who was ambitious to achieve something for herself. If I ever loved anyone again, it would be a woman who put her home and her husband before anything in the world. Unfortunately all the women I met had stars in their eyes which they hoped I would turn into reality. And then you came into my life.' He paused, and there was a long silence before he resumed. 'I saw the difference you made to Maggie; the way she responded to you—and the way everyone in the house responded to you—and I began to feel that at last I had found the one person I had been looking for.'

'You have,' she whispered, and came to stand beside him. 'Oh, Paul, can't you trust me?'

'Trust you?' he spat out. 'I wouldn't trust you with my dog, let alone my life!'

She fell back a step. 'You can't mean that?'

'I mean every word. You're a cheat and a liar. You lied your way into my heart.'

'I love you,' she cried. 'I never lied about that.'

'I don't believe you.' His eyes were bleak. 'I don't believe anything you've said to me. Go away, Sharon.'

She stared into his face. Had he still been furious she would have pleaded with him. But his calmness was more frightening than any anger could have been. She put out her

161

hand to him and he looked at it and then smiled, a hard bright smile.

'No, Sharon. It's over. I've woken up from my dream and found a nightmare in its place. If you have any feeling for me, you will pack at once and leave.'

'Very well,' she said huskily. 'But I do love you, Paul, and one day you'll realise it and regret what you've done.'

He shrugged and turned his back on her, and with a soundless cry she stumbled from the room.

CHAPTER THIRTEEN

EVEN weeks later, Sharon found it difficult to remember those few dreadful hours when she had packed and made arrangements to leave Pailings. Maggie's tears intermingled with her own, and her last sight of the house where she had found and lost her happiness was of a sobbing child standing on the stone steps.

During the long, slow journey to London she was able to regain some of her control, and she was dry-eyed and pale as a ghost when she finally knocked on the door of her brother's house later that afternoon and said she had lost her job.

One look at her face told Anne and Tim that there was more to it than that, but they did not question her, content to wait until she felt able to tell them the whole story, which she finally did the following day.

They were both horrified, not only by Tony's behaviour but by Paul's reception of it.

'If he really loved you,' Anne said, 'he'd know you're nothing like his first wife. Seems to me he's still locked up in the past.'

'That's true,' Sharon agreed bitterly. 'He thinks all singers are like Helga.'

'He may change his mind when he has a chance to cool down,' Tim interposed. 'My bet is that he'll be pounding this door down in a couple of days. He does have your address, I hope?'

Sharon nodded. She had left it with Maggie, more because the child had pleaded to have it than because she had considered Paul might wish to speak to her. But Tim's optimism about Paul proved unfounded, and when two weeks passed without a word from him, she knew she would never hear from him again. But this knowledge did not help her to erase him from her mind, and she realised that the only thing she could do was to find other work to fill her time, preferably away from London.

But first she went to see the specialist. He gave her the first ray of hope in what had been a totally grey world by telling her she could sing again in a month, and need have no fear that the trouble with her larynx would recur. It was unbelievably good news and she immediately called her agent, who promised to try and find her work for the coming operatic season beginning in September.

'I don't care what I do or where I go,' she informed him. 'I'd be quite happy to work abroad.'

'Who wouldn't?' he said drily. 'But you aren't yet ready for the Met!'

She laughed, and heard the sound as though it were coming from a stranger and not her own throat. It was the first time she had laughed at anything since leaving Pailings. 'I was thinking of a small company in Germany or Italy,' she explained. 'I have no trouble with languages and I'm not fussy about the pay. I just want to get away from England.'

'Is that the way for a confident singer to talk? You must work in London with a big company. We want the critics to hear you now, while you're young; not when you're old and fat!'

'At least make it old and thin,' she said wryly, and hung up, having just agreed to make no rash decision about her future.

Assuming it would be several months before her agent found her suitable work, she decided it was unfair to remain with Tim and Anne, and despite their protests announced

163

she would get herself a temporary job in a hotel.

'It's the holiday season, so it shouldn't be difficult,' she said, and proved it by immediately obtaining a position as a receptionist in a hotel on the south west coast.

It was a fortuitous move, for the same day that she got the job, Tim was asked to go to Canada for three months to supervise the new offices his company were opening in Vancouver. Since Anne and the twins would be allowed to accompany him, he had no hesitation in accepting the offer, and within a week the house was closed and its owners gone.

Sharon left for Cornwall at once, knowing that when she returned to London she would be returning to a completely different life. The future stretched ahead lonely and without love. It might hold success, as her agent and singing teacher prophesied, but it would not hold fulfilment; that could only come from one particular man, and he no longer wanted her.

Sharon had been working as a receptionist for three weeks when her agent, Leo Horan, telephoned her. He was so excited that his heavily accented voice—he hailed originally from mid-Europe—was even more difficult to understand than usual, and she had to ask him to repeat what he was telling her.

'It is the chance of a lifetime,' he said gutturally. 'If I had prayed for something sensational to happen for you, I wouldn't have had the nerve to pray for a thing like that!'

'A thing like what?' she demanded, laughing at his enthusiasm. 'You still haven't told me what it is.'

'The chance to sing Susanna in *The Marriage of Figaro*.'

The very name of the opera brought Paul so vividly to Sharon's mind that she was momentarily lost for words. But the silence did not worry Leo, who was busy telling her that the part was only available because the girl scheduled to sing it had been taken ill.

'But her bad luck is your good fortune,' he went on happily. 'It doesn't come to most new singers to get the chance to sing at Pailings so early on in their career.'

164

Pailings! The word sounded the death knell to Sharon's pleasure. She could never sing there. How upset Leo would be when she told him. If only she had had the forethought to tell him the whole story before coming to Cornwall. But somehow she had never envisaged getting the chance to sing in Paul's theatre and certainly never dreamt it would arise within a few weeks of leaving him.

'I have told the director you will be down to see him the day after tomorrow,' Leo said. 'You must come back to London at once and I will drive you to Sussex myself.'

'I can't sing at Pailings! I'll go anywhere else but there.'

'Are you crazy or something? This is a chance of a lifetime. If you are worried that you aren't good enough, I can assure you——'

'It isn't lack of confidence, Leo. It's just that. . . .' She hesitated, unwilling to put into words all that had happened between herself and Paul, yet knowing she owed Max some explanation for her behaviour. 'I—er—I know Paul Sanderson,' she said jerkily, 'and we've—we've quarrelled. He'll never let me sing in his theatre.'

'Sanderson isn't the sort of man to let a personal quarrel stand in the way of his company. If you are the right person for the part, he will take you.'

'He won't. He will never allow me to sing for his opera company.'

'You must have had one hell of a quarrel!' The Americanism, coupled with Leo's accent, sounded quaint. 'You must know Sanderson extremely well if you have had such a row with him. I didn't even realise you were on speaking terms—let alone non-speaking terms!'

'I suppose I should have told you,' she apologised, 'but I never thought the situation would arise.'

'That's what comes from having a first-class agent like me!'

Sharon conceded the point and then reiterated the impossibility of taking up the offer. 'The minute Paul saw me, he'd throw me out!'

'He couldn't. He is in America. He had to go over to

settle some details about a tour the company is doing there in the winter, and he won't be back for three weeks. By that time you will have made your debut and left. It is only for three performances. After that, they have engaged someone from Vienna. Please, Sharon, I beg you to listen to me. Sanderson won't know you have been to Pailings until you have gone!'

'I can't do it, Leo. I couldn't feel right singing at Pailings without Paul knowing.'

'A chance like this you can't turn down,' Leo said angrily. '*Figaro* is a new production this season and all the critics will be there to listen to it. You *have* to sing Susanna. I won't let you refuse.'

Sharon only half listened to Leo's pleading, her mind already winging thousands of miles across the Atlantic Ocean to Paul. Was he in New York or Los Angeles, and what was he doing at this moment? Probably sleeping, she thought, glancing at her watch and realising what time it was in America. Sleeping soundly while she was here aching for the sight of him and not knowing how she was going to live the rest of her life without him.

'So you see I am right,' Leo concluded. 'Now be a good girl and give in your notice. You're an opera singer, not a hotel receptionist.'

'Even if I agreed and went to Pailings, it would only be for a short time.'

'A week to rehearse and a week to sing. But after that you will receive other offers—I am sure of it. Now no more arguing. Pack up and come at once.'

As if in a dream, Sharon found herself obeying Leo, even though she knew she was doing the wrong thing. To go to Pailings again, even with Paul out of the country, would bring him so vividly close that it would re-awaken memories she was desperately trying to forget. Half-way through packing her cases she almost changed her mind, and only her recognition of what she owed to her agent prevented her from doing so. He had believed firmly in her talent from the moment he had heard her sing in that fateful perform-

166

ance of *Figaro* at college—and had nursed her along ever since, finding work for her when other singers had been jobless, and loaning her money when even he couldn't rustle up a singing engagement. And now he had managed—lord knew how—to get her the chance of singing the role of Susanna at Pailings. It was the opportunity of a lifetime, and not to take it would be foolhardy. As long as opera was going to be her career, she had to do all she could to further it. Paul would be furious when he found out, but by then she would have left Sussex.

At her first sight of the grey stone and timbered façade of Pailings Sharon felt she had never been away from it. It stood serene and untouched in the summer sunshine, and the lawns lay around it like a well kept carpet of green, interspersed here and there with overflowing flowerbeds. She was reminded vividly of the first time she had come here. How lighthearted she had been and how unaware that she would find the love of her life and also lose it again. Yet could one lose what one had never had? she thought dismally, and knew that if Paul had loved her as sincerely and deeply as she loved him, he would have understood why she had been afraid to tell him the truth about herself. No matter how unhappy his past had been, his love for her should have given him the ability to forgive.

With an effort she pushed the thought of him away. She had a great deal of work to do during the next few days and she must not live in the past. Until now she had been so busy with her personal emotions that she had given very little thought to the problems of singing in a new production with a conductor and cast she had never met. And most important of all, she would be using her voice again for the first time in six months. Though the specialist had assured her she need have no fear of using her voice, she knew she would not regain her full confidence until she had actually sung on a stage in a full performance. Only when she stood before a live audience and heard their applause would she feel she had resumed her career.

'Seen enough?' Leo asked. During the car journey down

167

from London he had learned something of what happened between Sharon and Paul, and without asking her, had brought the car to a stop outside the house instead of the theatre annexe.

'Quite enough,' she said firmly. 'Now stop your cathartic treatment and let's move on.'

With a grunt he swung the wheel and went back down the drive, turning right to stop outside the entrance to the theatre. He could not hide his pleasure nor excitement and he was half-way across the foyer before Sharon herself came in through the door.

The lights were on, although the auditorium itself was in darkness, but she could make out several people sitting in the stalls and recognised the director, who was on stage talking to a couple of singers. She also recognised several of the cast and for the first time remembered with a sense of shock that Tony would still be here, and singing opposite her. What a surprise he would get when he saw her! As the thought came into her mind he appeared from the wings, but because of the lights on stage he did not see her in the auditorium, and she watched him unnoticed, thinking how different her future might have been had she been able to tell Paul the truth about herself before he had learned it from Tony and Honor.

'Go on to the stage and meet the director,' Leo whispered, 'and stop looking worried. You will be wonderful.'

'Keep saying it, Leo, I need your confidence.'

He gave her a quizzical look but made no comment, and she followed him down the sloping aisle and up the steps at the side of the stage. The director recognised her at once, and regarded her with such astonishment that Sharon could not help smiling. The amusement lessened her nervousness, as did Tony's shout of welcome.

'Sharon!' he exclaimed. 'By all that's wonderful! I never thought to see you here again. Has——'

'I'm singing Susanna,' she interrupted before he could assume that she had come here at Paul's personal behest.

He looked astonished but had no chance to question her,

168

for the director immediately launched into a discussion of her part and was still talking as he called over the wardrobe mistress and arranged for her to be fitted for her costumes.

'I will go through the role with you alone this evening,' he said as she made her way towards the wings. 'We have already been rehearsing for a fortnight, so you will have a lot to catch up on.'

'Have you made much change in the interpretation?' she asked. 'I understand it's a new production.'

'I have broadened the character of the Countess,' he explained, 'but I haven't done too much with Susanna. As you know, Teresa Vicenti was singing the role and, though she has a wonderful voice, she acts like a plank of wood!'

'I'm not too bad as an actress,' Sharon said with the return of some of her confidence. 'And I'm willing to rehearse as many hours as you have the time to give me.'

'I'll hold you to that.' He touched her on the shoulder. 'So be prepared for some hard work.'

The warning was not an idle one, for during the next week she worked harder than she would have believed possible. Her only leisure was between six and eight in the evening, and she spent this time with Maggie. She had been uncertain whether or not to contact the little girl while she was here, and only the fact that Maggie would be hurt if she discovered Sharon was here without seeing her had prompted her to do so.

Anticipating many awkward questions as to why she had left so abruptly she was surprised that Maggie accepted her return with very little reference to her having gone away, and was oddly hurt that her absence should have been accepted so blithely. It was not until the end of the week, when the director decided to give her the evening off and she went across to the house to read Maggie a bedtime story, that the child explained the reason for her silence. Her father, it seemed, had carefully explained to her that he had had a personal quarrel with Sharon and had asked her to leave.

'But I knew Daddy would change his mind and have you

169

back again,' Maggie said. 'You just have to wait for him to get over his temper.'

Sharon wished that this was true, but forbore to say so. Within a fortnight she would be leaving here again, and soon after that Maggie would be going to her new school. Once among friends of her own age she would forget her old associations, no matter how happy they had been.

'I can't understand why Daddy didn't tell me you were coming back,' Maggie continued, as she clambered into bed and patted the side of it for Sharon to sit next to her.

'He didn't know.' The words popped out without Sharon meaning to say them, and she quickly picked up a book from the bedside table and thumbed through the pages. But Maggie pounced on the comment.

'You mean Daddy doesn't know you're here? That he's still cross with you?'

'Your father isn't cross with me,' Sharon lied. 'We just had—we just had a difference of opinion.'

'But Daddy likes you.'

'And I like your father,' Sharon said as composedly as she could. 'Now what story do you want me to read?'

'Will you be here when Daddy gets back from America?' Maggie asked, ignoring the question.

'I don't think so.'

'But you can't go away without seeing him again.'

'Your father doesn't want to see me again.'

'But if he isn't cross with you, why can't you wait and see him? I'm sure he——'

'Maggie, please,' Sharon's voice was ragged. 'Let's not talk about it any more.'

'But I *want* you to see him, I'm *sure* he isn't still mad at you. Please don't go away again.'

Maggie's lips trembled and Sharon pulled the thin figure close. 'Darling, don't cry; and listen to me carefully. I came back to Pailings to sing in *The Marriage of Figaro*. Your father doesn't know I'm here. You see, I'm afraid he's still annoyed with me and—and as soon as I've finished singing the role of Susanna, I'll be going back to London.'

170

'Won't I ever see you again?'

'Of course you will. I'll write to you when you're at school and send you tuckboxes.'

'I don't care about food,' Maggie cried, and burst into tears. 'I want to see *you*.' She flung her thin arms around Sharon's neck. 'I love you and I want you to stay with me.'

Sharon hugged the child close, dismayed at how quickly Maggie had twined her way into her heart. 'I love you too,' she said thickly, 'and I *will* keep in touch with you, I promise.'

Satisfied, Maggie leaned against the pillows and motioned Sharon to begin reading. It was *Alice in Wonderland*, but Alice, for all her precociousness, seemed very dumb when compared with Maggie, and Sharon thought how intrigued Lewis Carroll would have been had he been able to meet her. Heaven alone knew how different the story of Alice would have been if he had!

It was almost an hour later before she was finally able to leave the bedroom, and only then after she had promised to make arrangements for Maggie to watch the first performance of the opera.

'I've never seen you on the stage,' the little girl said sleepily. 'I can't believe you're really a singer. I always think of you as my friend.'

'I'm your singing friend!'

Maggie giggled, and burrowed sleepily into her pillow, though Sharon heard the ominous sound of bedsprings creak as she closed the door. What prank was she getting up to now? she speculated, but decided it could be nothing worse than getting herself another book to read.

As she left the house she glanced up to the first floor. Sure enough, the light was on in Maggie's bedroom. Still, it was holiday time, and without school to go to in the morning, it would not do the child any harm if she wished to stay up later. She had little enough pleasure in her life, living in a house of adults with a father who had turned his hobby into an obsession and was away as much as he was at home.

171

The thought of how different things could have been was such a sobering thought that her earlier mood of contentment vanished. But contentment was too strong a word to describe her earlier feelings; apathy was more apt, apathy and numbness.

'A penny for your thoughts?'

With a jerk, she looked up to see Tony on the path in front of her, and together they continued across the lawn to the new annexe where visiting singers were housed. Tony, here for the entire season, resided in the old wing, and he asked Sharon to join him there for a drink.

'Not tonight,' she sighed. 'I want to go to bed early.'

'Wernher working you hard, eh?'

'That's what I'm here for.'

'Your voice is better than ever,' Tony said. 'My bet is that you will stop the show!'

She laughed at the expression. 'I like the flattery, even though it doesn't happen to be true.'

'It *is* true,' he persisted. 'You are one of the best Susannas I have heard. In fact, your voice is too good for the part. You should be singing the Countess.'

'I must tell that to Leo.'

'He was the one who told me.'

At this she was genuinely surprised and, seeing it, Tony nodded. 'The director wants you to come down again next season,' he said quietly. 'Surely you know how pleased he is with you?'

'I didn't realise he was as pleased as all that.'

'Because you aren't using your head. All your thoughts are with Paul Sanderson.'

She quickened her pace and he kept in step with her.

'Don't be cross with me for talking about him, Sharon. We can't pretend he doesn't exist. I would give anything if I could undo my stupid behaviour.'

'Forget it.'

'But it was all my fault. If it hadn't been for me, Honor would never——'

'Forget it,' she repeated loudly. 'I don't want to talk

about it. Paul and I are through.'

'But you still love him.'

'He doesn't love me.' They continued to walk in silence and Sharon was glad when she saw the annexe looming up in front of her.

'I suppose you know that Honor is with him in America,' Tony said suddenly.

Sharon stumbled and righted herself. 'I didn't know,' she said carefully, and marvelled she could keep her voice so prosaic. 'That should at least prove to you that I mean nothing to Paul.'

'Because he is with Honor? Don't be naïve. What has one thing got to do with another? A man needs a woman, Sharon, and if he——'

'I don't want to discuss it!' she cried, and mumbling a quick goodnight, fled into the foyer.

So Honor had gone to America with Paul; was with him at this very moment. The knowledge put paid to any hopes she might still have had that he might be thinking of herself and missing her. She climbed the stairs to her bedroom and closed the door behind her. How easily a man could find solace in another woman's arms; content to settle for passion if he could not have true love. If only *she* were as easy to satisfy. Sighing, he began to undress. If only he had not turned to Honor Macklin for comfort. The very woman whose culpability had brought about the end of their happiness. If she needed anything to make her put Paul out of her mind, the knowledge that he was in America with Honor should be more than enough.

But wishing to forget someone did not mean that the wish would come true, and Paul was as vivid in her imagination when she woke up the next morning as he had been when she had gone to bed. Only when she was on stage singing could she forget him, and because of this she worked continually, co-opting Tony's aid when the director was busy with other members of the cast.

The day before the premiere of the new production, Wernher ordered her to rest.

'If you rehearse any more, you will be as stale as yesterday's doughnut! I forbid you to sing it again until tomorrow night.'

'Just once more,' she pleaded.

'No,' he said firmly, and swinging round upon Tony, ordered him to take her out to dinner. 'Up to London, if you like, provided you don't come back on the last train. But just get her to stop thinking about the part for the next twelve hours.'

'An excellent suggestion,' Tony beamed in Sharon's direction. 'We still haven't tried that Italian restaurant in Haywards Heath.'

His words brought back an immediate memory of the last time he had offered to take her there. Her thoughts must have been apparent on her face, for Tony went scarlet.

'We will go to London,' he said hastily.

'We will go to that Italian restaurant,' she replied with a composure she did not feel. 'As you've already told me, one can't keep living in the past.'

Immediately he brightened, accepting at face value words which to her were a total lie. She could never live except in the past; for in the present and the future she had no life; there would never be a life for her when Paul was not there to share it.

It was well after midnight when she and Tony returned from their dinner. The evening had passed surprisingly quickly, for he had set out to entertain her, and for a couple of hours she had not thought of Paul at all. But returning to Pailings and seeing his house loom majestically in the darkness, she was again reminded of him, and knew she would have no peace while she was living here. Still, by the end of the week she would be gone, and a singer of international repute would be coming to take her place, despite the fact that Wernher was ecstatic about her voice.

'But we are already committed to someone else for this season,' he had said. 'So you will not be able to sing here until next year.'

Sharon had forborne to tell him that even next year she

174

would not be able to sing at Pailings. He would find out for himself when he put her name forward to Paul.

'You are not nervous about tomorrow night, are you?' Tony interrupted her thoughts.

'I feel numb,' she confessed. 'I will probably be petrified tomorrow night.'

'You don't need to be. I have never heard you in better voice. You have a great future ahead of you. You know that, don't you?'

He was echoing what she had already been told, and though she knew she should be elated, she could feel nothing but apathy. She was obviously one of those women who believed the world well lost for love.

Her apathy lessened as the hour of her debut grew nearer.

She had kept her promise to Maggie and had arranged for her to watch the performance, and she telephoned her to make sure that Goodwin or someone else from the staff would accompany her through the grounds and then come back to take her home again.

'I don't need anyone to go with me,' Maggie asserted. 'I'll cut through the kitchen garden and round the back.'

'You're not to go wandering on your own at night.'

'But it's my home,' Maggie protested.

'There are lots of strangers here. Now promise me, Maggie, or I'll worry.'

'Don't worry, Sharon,' Maggie said, and gave an excited giggle. 'I promise I won't come on my own.'

'I hope you're not plotting some mischief?' Sharon asked suspiciously.

'Of course not. I've been good for weeks and weeks.'

'Well, mind you stay that way—at least until the performance is over tonight.'

'Are you scared?' Maggie asked.

'To death,' Sharon replied, and heard another giggle as she put down the receiver. A few more hours and she would be making her singing debut at Pailings, listened to by some of the most stringent critics in the country. The palms of her hand grew damp at the thought, and to combat her nerves she went to her dressing room earlier than was necessary. Once among the familiar sight and smell of greasepaint she felt better, and almost immediately began to feel herself as Susanna: cheeky, witty, lighthearted Susanna, who dreamed only of marriage to Figaro and a happy future with him.

Long before she was due on stage, Sharon was waiting in the wings. As always there was the usual backstage excitement and drama. The somewhat Junoesque Swedish woman singing the Countess displayed an unusual and un-Swedish tantrum, while the Count, normally a jovial Scotsman, complained so bitterly about his costume being too tight that the wardrobe mistress was reduced to tears. Luckily Tony was his normal ebullient self, and kept peering through a chink in the curtains to keep Sharon informed as to the state of the audience as they filed in and took their seats.

'Bertram Drew is here.' He proclaimed the arrival of the most august of the critics. 'And so is what's-his-name from *The Times*.'

'Don't tell me any more,' Sharon begged. 'The butterflies in my stomach are turning into dragons!'

Tony chuckled. 'Baxter has just come in. He's the bloke from the B.B.C.—good heavens, he's with——' he stopped abruptly and she waited for him to continue.

'Who is it?' she asked. 'Anyone important?'

'No one for you to bother your head about.' He let the curtain fall into place. 'The orchestra is coming in now. Five more minutes and the overture will begin.'

'Is Maggie here yet?'

'Wernher has put an extra seat in one of the boxes.'

She went to move past Tony to look through the curtain, but he caught her arm and pulled her back.

'You must not look at the audience,' he grumbled. 'It's supposed to be unlucky to do so before your first performance.'

Well acquainted though she was with the superstitious

lore of the theatre, this was one that Sharon had not yet heard, and she impatiently went to shake off his hand. But he kept tight hold of her and propelled her into the side of the wings.

'Don't worry about Maggie. She's perfectly settled.'

Placated, yet still faintly perturbed, Sharon waited in the wings. Behind them more of the cast had gathered, and a couple of scene-shifters edged on to the stage while a young woman rushed forward to make sure that the length of material, behind which one of the singers would be hiding during part of the first act, had been placed on the back of the armchair. Wernher went on stage for a final look round, declared himself satisfied with what he saw and then came over towards Sharon.

'I am glad to see you aren't nervous,' he said, taking her calm at face value. 'Just remember to keep up the tempo in your first duet, and don't gabble the recitative.'

She nodded and he patted her reassuringly on the shoulder.

'Paul is out front, so you are in luck. If he rates your performance tonight as highly as I do, he'll be signing you up here and now for next season.'

Sharon swallowed hard, not sure she had heard correctly. 'Did you say Paul is *here*? But I thought he was in America.'

'So did everyone else. He flew in unexpectedly this afternoon. Got here less than an hour ago, in fact.'

'Why?' She clutched the director's arm. 'Does he know it's *me* who's singing Susanna? Have you seen him since he got home?'

'Of course he knows you're singing Susanna. He rang up and spoke to me as soon as he arrived. I haven't seen him, though. We only spoke on the telephone.'

'What did he say? Was he angry?'

'Why should he be angry?' Wernher gave her a shake. 'What is the matter with you, my dear? You're pale enough to go haunting someone! I'll get you a brandy.'

'I don't want anything,' she said shakily. 'I feel fine.'

177

'You mustn't worry about Paul hearing you. You should be thrilled.'

'I am—I'm not sure.' She was incoherent but could not make the effort to be logical. Her thoughts were jumbled into a kaleidoscope of joy and fear, pain and pleasure. Much as he hated to have her sing at Pailings, Paul was unable to stop it, and she had the triumph of knowing he was going to watch her make the most important debut of her life to date. Apart from that fateful tape, he had never heard her sing, and tonight she was going to sing for him alone. Even though he despised her he was too much of a professional to hear her voice and refrain from assessing its quality. And because of this, he would be forced to judge her for himself.

Miraculously all her fears vanished and she was bolstered by a fierce determination to make him appreciate her talent; to make him see that the years of work had not been vain ones, and that her belief in herself was not based on conceit but on the conviction that her voice was a wonderful gift which had been given to her and which she had a duty to cherish and to use.

In the pit the orchestra tuned up. There was no longer any sound from the auditorium save for an occasional cough. Then there was a momentary silence and the hushed expectancy that always seemed to come before the overture began. Sharon caught her breath and waited, knowing that soon the curtains would part and she would be facing her greatest test. She smoothed the skirts of her pert dress and made sure that the cap on her hair was securely pinned.

'You're the loveliest Susanna I've seen in years,' her dresser had said earlier, and she gained some comfort from the knowledge that Paul would not only hear her in good voice but would see her looking lovely too. She drew a deep breath and moved on to the stage, sending up a swift prayer as the overture ended, the curtains swished back and the opera began.

Throughout the performance Sharon remained Susanna, not even touching reality during the lengthy interval which enabled the audience to have dinner. Declining anything to drink, she sat in her dressing room glancing through a score she already knew by heart, and thinking over the performance that still lay ahead of her.

She knew Paul was sitting in his box to the left of the stage, but she had resolutely refused to glance in his direction when she had taken the vociferous curtain calls at the end of the first act. It was bad enough knowing he was listening to her without having the added drama of seeing him. Yet meet him she must, if she intended to sing out the rest of her short contract here. Somehow she could not believe he would make her leave before the end of the week. No matter how deeply he disliked her, he was too much of a professional to let his personal feelings get the better of him.

'Five-minutes, Miss,' a voice informed her, and she peered into the mirror and applied a light dusting of powder to her face. How bright her eyes were with excitement and unshed tears. Quickly she turned away from her reflection, afraid of what else she might read in her eyes, and sped down the corridor to the wings. What a pleasure it was to work in a theatre where everything had been meticulously planned. There were no draughty areas to cross to get from her dressing room to the stage, no narrow corridors to traverse in difficult costumes and no jostling for position in the wings in order to get a view of what was happening on stage. Not only were the audience well catered for, with comfortable seats and magnificent acoustics, but the singers were well catered for too.

'I have just been speaking to Bertram Drew.' Wernher came to stand beside her, his broad face creased in a smile. 'He wanted to know everything about you. He couldn't understand why he had never heard you sing before.'

'What did you tell him?'

'That Paul discovered you.' His smile became more pronounced. 'It is good to encourage a wide belief in Paul's legendary ability to discover new operatic talent!'

179

'He might not be so pleased to be credited with discovering *me*,' she retorted.

Wernher chuckled. 'On the contrary, my dear, he was with Drew when I made the statement, and when I left them together, he was busily telling Drew exactly where he found you.'

'I would have liked to hear that story,' she said drily, and felt an inexplicable anger against Paul. How callously he had dismissed her, and how easily he was now assuming the role of her discoverer, which Leo had designated for him.

But there was not time for further thought. The audience had resumed their places and the house lights were already dimming for the second time. What irony it was to go on stage and be lighthearted and gay when all she wanted to do was to weep. She drew a deep breath, and became aware that Tony was next to her. She knew he was waiting for her to mention Paul, but she could not bring herself to do so. Later on she would have to talk of his unexpected return home, but for the moment she must concentrate on the beautiful music. Sad music this time, as the Countess bewailed the infidelity of her husband. Unbidden, a picture of Honor flashed before her, and she would have given a great deal to know if the woman was with Paul.

'You're on,' Wernher hissed in her ear, and she parted her lips in a smile and stepped into the warmth of the spotlights.

An hour and ten curtain calls later, Sharon still found it difficult to return to earth. She had received a standing ovation; one given to few singers so early on in their career, and she was still overwhelmed by it and unable to credit her luck.

'Not luck,' Wernher stated. 'Recognition of a great voice. This is only the beginning for you. Today it is Pailings, tomorrow it will be the Metropolitan, La Scala, Covent Garden.'

'I'll settle for Covent Garden,' she whispered.

'You can take that as read. Leo will be fighting them off.'

180

'That's one battle he's going to love!' she said with a tremulous laugh, and moved in the direction of her dressing room.

'Don't be long changing, Sharon. Paul has invited us to his house for a champagne supper.'

She stopped and clutched at the wall. 'You'd better make my apologies,' she said with commendable calm. 'I couldn't face anyone tonight.'

'You will feel better once you have relaxed and taken off your make-up.'

'No,' she repeated. 'I don't want to go.' Aware of the director's surprise, she searched for a further excuse. 'I have a splitting headache. I really can't face any more people.'

'Do you have any aspirins?'

She nodded. 'I'll feel better once I lie down.'

'I will be in to see you before I leave the theatre.'

'I won't change my mind about the party.'

'Who said anything about the party?' he replied. 'I am concerned about *you*.'

He strode away and Sharon sped to her dressing room. Too enervated to get out of her costume, she sat on the dressing-table stool, her shiny pink satin skirts billowing around her, so that she felt she was sitting in the centre of an eiderdown. Her refusal to go to Paul's house would cause comment among the cast, but she was beyond caring. She had to preserve her own dignity and calm and she was not sure she could do so if she came face to face with him tonight. But would she be any more composed tomorrow? She did not know the answer to that; all she knew was that she could not face him without preparing herself a little longer.

The headache she had lied about was slowly becoming a reality, and she put her hands to her temples and massaged them. It was hours since she had eaten anything, and though she had no appetite—nerves and her awareness of Paul's proximity had robbed her of that—she knew she would be ill if she did not swallow something. There was a

181

knock at the door and the dresser came in with a tray. On it was a glass of water and some tablets and a pot of tea and plate of sandwiches.

'I've been told to see you take the pills and eat the food,' the woman said. 'Every single sandwich!'

With a slight smile Sharon did as she was told, eating the sandwiches as quickly as she could. If she knew Wernher, he would give her half an hour to recover and then come and try to make her change her mind about going to Paul's party. Unable to face further discussion about it, she determined to be safely in her bedroom before he came in search for her. To this end she undressed with speed, nervously wiping off her make-up and flinging the tissues haphazardly on the floor. Without the glow of artificial colour her skin seemed inordinately pale, the blue shadows under her eyes looking more pronounced. Had Paul had sleepless nights too, since they had parted, or had his nights been too preoccupied with Honor? The thought evoked such painful images that she reached blindly for a cardigan and slipped it over her shoulders before making her way to the door.

The passageways were deserted, for most of the cast were still changing, and careful to avoid being seen, she sped to the stage door. Unlike a normal theatre there were no fans waiting outside. Pailings' audiences were too sophisticated to come and see their stars in such a fashion, and thankful for the anonymity this afforded her, Sharon crossed the wide expanse of gravel path and headed for the annexe.

Skirting the flowerbeds, their brilliant coloured blooms looking various shades of grey in the moonlight, she paused to breathe in the scent that was wafted in the air around her. A particularly fragrant clump of tobacco plants was near by, silvery white as the moon which shone on them, and she bent low to savour their bouquet. Only as she did so did she become aware of the more pungent aroma of Havana, and it needed no quiet step to tell her that Paul was in front of her. Slowly she straightened and looked at him, glad that their first meeting after so long should be in the moonlight, where thoughts could not be easily read and emotions could more easily be hidden.

'Hello, Paul,' she said evenly. 'I didn't expect to see you here.'

'That's my line, I think.'

Her mouth went dry at the calm measuredness of his tone. 'I hadn't—hadn't planned on coming here to sing,' she said jerkily. 'Leo—my agent—arranged it and—and I tried to refuse, but he—but it was very difficult.'

'I've already spoken to your agent,' Paul said. 'He left me in no doubt of your reluctance to come here.'

'I told him we had a quarrel,' she said awkwardly, 'but he doesn't know the whole story.'

'I'm glad.' Paul's voice was still expressionless. 'I wouldn't like anyone to know why I sent you away.'

'Naturally,' she said coldly. 'I understand Wernher has given you the credit for discovering me!' She saw his eyes narrow and knew he had not followed her remark. 'I believe it will give you the right sort of publicity for Pailings.'

'To hell with Pailings!' For the first time he spoke with vehemence. 'Do you think I give a damn about the opera company? It's you I'm concerned with. You and your future.'

'My agent can take care of my future,' she replied. 'And if you wish me to leave tomorrow I——'

'I don't ever want you to leave!' He reached out and gripped her arm, pulling her without further ado across the lawn and into a secluded arbour. A rustic bench stood there and she sank down on it, grateful for its support.

'Don't let's pretend any more, Sharon.' Paul's voice was no longer calm but swift and urgent, the words tumbling out unmonitored. 'I should never have sent you away. If the whole thing hadn't come as such a shock to me, I would never have done it. But everything happened so quickly that my reaction was automatic. I couldn't think of *you*— the person I knew you to be—all I could remember was Helga. I made the mistake of judging the future in terms of the past. If I hadn't done so, I would never have spoken to

183

you the way I did.'

They were words she had not expected to hear, and though she was glad of them, they did not bring her the happiness she had believed they would.

'Well?' he said huskily. 'Why are you sitting there so quietly? Don't you know what I'm trying to tell you? I love you and I want to spend the rest of my life making you happy.' He bent towards her, but she slithered across the bench and jumped to her feet.

'No, Paul, it's no use. It's too late.'

'What do you mean?'

'It's too late,' she repeated.

'But we love each other.' He stepped towards her. 'Or are you telling me you've changed your mind?'

'It's too late,' she said again, unable to deny her love for him, yet unable to accept all that he was offering.

'For heaven's sake, Sharon!' He caught her by the shoulders. 'Why are you staring at me like that? If you want to make me pay for the way I behaved to you——'

'Of course not!' she cried. 'But you can't come back into my life and begin where you left off. It's over. Finished!'

Still he did not let her go. 'I don't believe you. Not unless you look me in the face and tell me you don't love me.'

'It has nothing to do with love,' she whispered, head bent low. 'It has to do with faith.'

At this, his hands dropped away, though he still remained in front of her barring her escape. 'I don't understand. What has faith to do with it?'

'Without faith in a person, your love for them is meaningless.'

'Is that how you see my love for you—as meaningless?'

She moistened her lips and glanced over his shoulder, wishing she could escape from him.

'Well?' he demanded. 'You still haven't answered me.'

'Do I need to?' she burst out. 'Do you think I don't know the reason why you want me? And it has nothing to do with love!'

'Then why am I here?'

'Because you *need* me. You desire me, yet you hate me for it. You will always remember that I came into your life on a lie.'

'So it's only desire, is it?' Once again his hands were on her shoulders, hard as a vice. 'Do you think I'm so desperate for a woman's body that I'll settle for someone I hate?'

With each harsh word he shook her, making her teeth rattle and her hair tumble around her head. The false curls she had worn on stage and forgotten to unpin came free and fell to the ground. He looked so astonished that she giggled, and when she wanted to stop she found she could not do so. Laughter trembled on her lips and swirled up in her throat, emerging as a sharp peal of hysteria.

'Stop it!' he commanded, and shook her again. But she could not stop and her laughter grew louder still and higher. 'Stop it!' he ordered, and smacked his hand across her cheek.

The laughter died in her throat and the pain of his fingers brought tears to her eyes, which glittered there like diamonds.

'Darling,' he said huskily. 'Oh, darling, I don't want to hurt you.'

Before she could stop him he pulled her close and laid his mouth on hers, running his hands down the centre of her back and pressing her against him as though to reassure himself she was there. She tried to resist his touch, but it was a losing battle, and with a sigh she put her arms around his neck and clung to him.

'I love you,' he whispered against her throat. 'You don't know what my life has been like since you left.'

The words brought back the cold touch of reality and she tried to draw away, but though he let her move slightly he still kept his hold on her.

'You can't deny you love me,' he said huskily. 'It was in your eyes when you saw me tonight.'

'It still won't work, Paul.'

'Why do you say that?'

She hesitated, then plunged on. 'If you hadn't come back to Pailings and found me here, you would still be nursing

185

your hurt pride. You would still be as bitter towards me as you are to your first wife.'

'That's not true! You're as different from Helga as the sun from the moon. You're a woman, Sharon, a woman of flesh and blood. You have a glorious talent, but it hasn't stopped you from having a loving heart.'

'You didn't think that the last time you spoke to me.'

'I've already told you why I said what I did. I was angry and hurt. I couldn't think straight.'

'And you might not think straight when you see me again tomorrow.'

He bent forward to look searchingly into her face. 'Do you think I've been carried away by the shock of seeing you?'

'Haven't you? You can't deny it *was* a shock for you to come back to Pailings and find me there.'

'Oh no,' he said. 'I came back *because* you were here.'

'You knew?'

'Yes. I telephoned Maggie a couple of days ago and she told me. I would have come back at once except that I couldn't get away.'

'Why did you want to see me?' she asked, unwilling to take his words at face value. 'Were you angry to think I would come here behind your back?'

'I was angry to think you were here while I was away.' His voice grew deeper. 'I've been searching London for you for weeks, but no one knew where you were.'

For an instant she was filled with joy. Then logic returned and she made a disclaiming gesture. 'You couldn't have tried very hard, Paul. The agency who engaged me to come here had my address.'

'Maybe they did,' he said grimly, 'but by the time I got round to finding them, they'd closed for a month's holiday.' He pulled Sharon down on the bench again and kept his hands tightly on hers, as though afraid she would get up and run away. 'Let me explain,' he said quietly. 'I can see you won't believe me until I do.'

In precise and careful tones, the very preciseness hiding the anguish he must have experienced, he told of the bitterness he had felt when he first learned she was a singer and had come to look after Maggie without telling him the truth. 'For the first few weeks after I sent you away I lived through hell. But then I began to see it was a hell of my own making. I started to think about you—you as I knew you to be—a warm, lovable girl who had turned my monster of a daughter into a lovable child, and me from a miserable cur into a man who could start thinking of his own future again. That was when I started to look for you. But by then the domestic agency had closed for its annual holiday. I even went round all the theatrical agents, but none of them had heard of you. I never thought of contacting Leo,' he concluded. 'He only takes the top singers.'

'I'm the only unknown he has on his books,' she confessed.

'You won't be unknown after tonight.' There was a tone in Paul's voice that made her look at him more closely. But he seemed unaware of it and went on talking. 'When I learned from Maggie that you were here, I knew I couldn't run the risk of your leaving before I got back. That's why I flew home as soon as I could. I'll have to return to New York to finalise my arrangements, but I'm hoping you'll let me make it a honeymoon.'

She trembled so violently that she could not speak, but he understood her silence, for he pulled her back against his chest and rested his lips on her temples.

'Will you forgive me for the way I behaved? I'll never be jealous of you again, my darling, at least not of your career!'

She stirred in his arms and the question she had always meant to ask him was finally said. 'Would you like me to give it up? I will if you want me to. My life with you is more important to me than my voice.'

The look of incredulity in his eyes died as the love he felt for her blazed out. 'You—you would do that for me?' he said jerkily. 'Give everything up when you—when you're on the eve of your career?'

'I love you, Paul. My happiness is with you, not with singing.'

'But I want you to sing! So long as it doesn't take you away from me; so long as I can be with you and share your success.'

Her sigh was one of pure contentment. 'When I woke up this morning I never thought the day would end like this.'

'I did,' he said whimsically. 'Even when you turned on me like a virago a moment ago, I knew I was never going to let you escape from me again.'

'How right you were,' she said with a shaky laugh, and then because candour was one of her characteristics, she had to know about Honor. 'Not that I'm jealous of her still,' she said untruthfully, 'but——'

'Little liar!' he interrupted, giving her a tender shake. 'But you have no reason to be jealous—neither now or for my past. At one time I did consider marrying her, but I could never bring myself to the point of proposing. There was a hardness in her which repelled me.'

'But you were with her in New York.'

'She came to New York because she knew I was there,' he corrected, 'and if you mean what I think you mean, let me assure you that you're wrong.'

Sharon's jealousy dissolved as though it had never existed. 'Oh, Paul, I'm so happy I could cry,' she said, and flung her arms around him again.

'I would rather you said you were so happy you could sing.'

'I've already sung for my supper!'

'Then let me give it to you!' He pulled her to her feet but kept his arms around her, his fingers cupping the side of her breast. 'There's so much more I want to give you,' he murmured. 'But we must get the licence first.'

'When?' she asked shamelessly.

'Tomorrow. Then we can be married by the weekend.'

'My own marriage instead of a make-believe one.'

'A marriage that won't end when the curtain comes down,' he said seriously, and catching her hand he led her across the lawn and into his home. 'And into my heart,' he said, divining her thoughts, 'for ever.'

Best Seller Romances

Romances you have loved

Mills & Boon Best Seller Romances are the love stories that have proved particularly popular with our readers. They really are "back by popular demand." These are the other titles to look out for this month.

THERE CAME A TYRANT
by Anne Hampson

Simoni knew she would just never get on with Kent Travers. He was tyrannical, unreasonable, for ever finding fault with her and her work. Thank goodness they would both soon be leaving their jobs and she need never have anything to do with him again. But that was where Simoni was wrong!

COME RUNNING
by Anne Mather

Darrell Anderson had fallen in love with Matthew Lawford, who was married – unhappily, but married none the less. She knew that she would still go to him on any terms he chose to name – but was there any chance of happiness for them, even if she did?

Mills & Boon

ADAM'S RIB
by Margaret Rome

Tammy Maxwell and Adam Fox had married for nothing but expediency – and now here she was, installed in his remote house in the Cumbrian Fells; realising, too late, that she had fallen in love with him – and that he felt nothing for her but contempt. What should she do now?

FLIGHT INTO YESTERDAY
by Margaret Way

To Lang Frazer, Natalie was just a spoilt, heartless girl who revelled in hurting her father and her stepmother Britt. But Natalie saw Britt as the woman who had ruined her relationship with her father. How could she see Lang with anything but resentment? What did he know about it all anyway?

THE SUN TOWER
by Violet Winspear

Dina Caslyn had been a part of rich Californian society for most of her life, and her marriage to Bay Bigelow would consolidate her position. Then the mysterious Raf Ventura kept crossing her path, and making it clear that he wanted her himself. But there was too much to put at risk. Dina didn't dare to fall in love with him . . .

the rose of romance